AN UNEXPECTED MATCH
Making a Family Series, Book Two

BARBARA MCMAHON

An Unexpected Match
Copyright © 2024 Barbara McMahon
All Rights Reserved

Chapter One

"The thing is, Arden, I hear Brendan Ferguson is a by-the-book kind of guy."

Arden Glover looked at her best friend and temporary roommate in surprise. Slowly buttoning her brocade vest, she shrugged.

"Then I'll give him a by-the-book kind of interview."

Patti hooted with laughter. "You? By the book?"

Arden grinned and studied her reflection in the mirror. This was the third outfit she'd tried on. If she didn't decide soon, she'd be late for the interview and then it wouldn't matter if it went by the book or not.

This would have to do. The dark blue skirt brushed the tops of her knees. The multicolored, jewel-tone brocade vest contrasted nicely. It was too hot to bother with a blouse. May had been warm all month and her legs were tanned enough to forego stockings.

Eyes twinkling, she glanced slyly at her friend.

"You doubt I can pull it off?"

"Somehow, I can't imagine you as a follow-the-rules kind

of person. Of course, you could be hiding that aspect from me. We've only known each other a few years."

Patti grinned at her own joke.

Arden looked at her in mock surprise.

"I'm amazed you doubt me. I never speed when driving. I balance my checkbook every month, and I always look both ways before crossing the street. How much more follow-the-rules could I be?"

"You start work at four in the afternoon and don't stop until four in the morning, then sleep all day. You eat pizza for breakfast and pancakes for dinner. And you keep your great-aunts out long past curfew. How's that for starters?" Patti said.

"Curfew for women in their eighties is ridiculous. And it was only that one time. Besides, I like pizza anytime of the day. What should I do with my hair?"

Slipping on her sandals, Arden studied her hair. How should she fix that? The wild tangle of blond curls was the bane of her existence. All her life she'd longed for glossy straight dark hair. Of course, she'd also longed to be petite with an air of fragility, too. None of her wishes along those lines had come true. She believed she had accepted the fact that she was tall and slender with wild hair. But the old dreams sometimes surfaced. Today was one of those times.

"Wear it pulled back, with a bow that picks up the blue in the vest," Patti suggested, stretching and sitting up on the edge of the bed. "Worn loose, you look about fifteen and he won't think you're old enough to watch his little girls. If you do anything elaborate, he'll think you're too sophisticated. I don't know why you have to do this, anyway. You're welcome to stay here. I've told you that a dozen times."

Arden smiled at her friend.

"You've been a lifesaver. I don't know where I would have gone when the aunts moved into that retirement home if I couldn't have come here. But what works for the two of us while Doug is out on deployment won't work when he gets home. You won't want a third around and you know it."

Patti's husband was a submariner currently finishing a three-month cruise and scheduled to return before the first of June. Arden knew how much the newlyweds would want their own space. She was determined to find something by then that would allow her to move into a place of her own.

Patti blushed and shrugged, but stars filled her eyes. "I guess."

"I know for sure Doug won't want me here. If I get this job, it'll solve all my worries. The ad mentioned a place to live. Combine that with the tidy salary offered and the kind of work I can do while I continue with school, it's all absolutely perfect."

"If it sounds too good to be true, it probably is. Besides, you'll never make it. He's a real rules-and-regulations kind of guy," Patti warned.

"For heaven's sake, Patti. Brendan Ferguson is a security

expert. They're the kings of spontaneity having to cover all contingencies. How by-the-rules can he be? My understanding of the breed is that they counter any attempts at security breaches, foil kidnappings of rich businessmen, think fast on their feet and still come out ahead. Doesn't sound like he crosses every t and dots every I to me."

Studying the effect of her hair, Arden nodded, clasping on a blue bow.

"I guess this will work."

"You'll knock him dead," her friend said loyally.

"Oh, that's great. I need him alive to hire me."

Arden arrived at the high-rise office building for her interview well before her scheduled time. She refused to acknowledge the nervousness that plagued her as she stepped into the elevator. Instead, she concentrated on how best to make a good first impression. Patti had seen the discrete job posting on the bulletin board in the building's coffee shop, and told Arden about it. Now she was about to meet the man who needed a nanny for his preschool daughters.

Stepping off the elevator a few moments later, she glanced around with interest. She'd never been in a high-security company before and was curious to see if she could spot any of the devices they probably used as a matter of course. They must have monitors, video cameras, laser beams everywhere.

Instead, she frowned at the austere reception area. She could detect nothing to differentiate it from any other office she'd been in, except for the bland paint, the blank walls with no art.

Color and lines and designs fascinated her. Maybe she ought to offer a few paintings to enhance the area.

She almost laughed at the image that produced. As if an expert hostage negotiator, an anti-infiltrating security engineer cared what she thought of the walls in his offices. For all she knew, he kept the walls bare for a reason.

It couldn't have been a lack of money; his company's services were reported to be in high demand, despite costing a bundle. Patti had shared that information when telling her about the job posting.

The receptionist greeted Arden and immediately ushered her into an empty conference room.

"Mr. Ferguson will be right with you," she said after offering Arden some coffee.

Arden declined the coffee and moved to sit in one of the chairs against the wall, leaving the chairs encircling the enormous oval table empty. The view from the windows faced east. Even though the Chesapeake Bay was blocks away, with a dozen other high-rise office buildings between, she looked in a vain hope to glimpse the water.

Two minutes later, a tall, dark-haired man strode in, carrying a folder. The air seemed suddenly charged. Arden blinked and tried a smile. Her heart began pounding.

"Arden Glover?" he asked, stopping just inside the door.

"I'm Brendan Ferguson."

He stood ramrod straight and topped her own five-feet-ten inches by a good half foot or more. His dark gray suit was superbly tailored, his pristine white shirt a crisp, clean contrast. The deep maroon tie gave the final fillip to power. He seemed to radiate energy.

She almost jumped up and snapped a salute. Gripping her purse, she resisted the urge, suspecting he might not find any humor in such an action.

"How do you do?" she replied, conscious of Patti's advice.

His glance roamed quickly over her, then he dropped his gaze to the folder. Opening it as he walked slowly to the table, he scanned the page inside.

A lean, mean, fighting machine echoed in Arden's mind as she watched him, her artist's eye delighting in the lines and contrasts she saw. She could picture him as a pagan warrior. A fighter. Protector. Not wearing a suit, of course, but in leather, or animal skins, or little at all.

She suddenly itched to sketch the man. She'd pose him with a lance, or a sword, chest bare daring the enemy to do his worst, knowing he'd be victorious no matter what came his way.

The suit couldn't hide the breadth of his shoulders, the long length of his legs. She glimpsed a well-toned form beneath his shirt when the suit jacket opened–rock-hard muscles she'd bet. Sculpting their shape, hiding nothing, she could bring his form to life in passionate detail.

The deep tan that darkened his skin went with the midnight black of his hair. Did he spend a good portion of his life outdoors? No office worker acquired such a dark hue. His eyes were gunmetal gray, cool and assessing. His lips were full, but held in a tight line.

What would soften them? Laughter, certainly. Passion?

What about when he kissed a woman, whispered sweet words of love in her ear?

Arden let her gaze dance over the strong contour before her. Deltoids, pecs and biceps were covered, but her imagination ran rampant. She bet they were toned and developed until she knew a quarter would bounce off if dropped. No, wait, that was for beds, tightly made beds that quarters bounced on.

Thinking of beds, she wondered what he'd look like in one stretched out beneath a light sheet. She suspected he eschewed clothing while sleeping. Was he tanned all over or only on his face? Would his chest be a lighter hue or that same rich teak? Did he sleep on his stomach or on his back? Did he sprawl over the entire bed or keep to one side?

Suddenly Arden realized the silence had gone on for quite some time. Too long. Raising her gaze in confusion, she saw he was staring at her. Had he said something? Asked her a question?

Read her mind?

Slowly, she tried a smile, but the flicker of heat deep inside startled her. Baffled her. What was going on? Just because he had a body that most men would envy, and every woman alive would drool over, was no reason for her to feel any specific attraction. She loved all forms of art.

And he could sure be considered a masterpiece, her mind whispered.

Her heart kicked hard against her chest.

Nerves. She really wanted this job.

Brendan Ferguson laid the folder on the conference table and leaned against the edge, crossing his arms across his chest, his gaze never wavering from her.

Her skin prickled, and her heart rate increased. Suddenly she felt deliciously feminine, as if in response to the call of a primal male.

Blinking, Arden drew in a sharp breath. She was here for a by-the-book interview, not to create fantasies about the man. She sat even straighter in her chair.

"You have a rather eclectic work history," he said slowly. "Over the last seven years, you've had seven different jobs. Waitress, library aide, flower shop delivery person, day-care worker, lifeguard at the beach, a Merry Maid, whatever that is, and hospice work. Not one job lasted longer than eight months."

Arden nodded.

"Nothing shows me you have training for childcare. And

I need someone I can count on for longer than a few months."

He flipped the folder closed as if ending the interview.

Panic flared. Arden stood and reached out her hand, not quite touching him, but coming close enough to feel the heat radiating from his body. Recognizing a matching heat in her own, she dropped her arm and raised her chin. She couldn't let the interview fizzle out like that.

"I can explain the eclectic work history. I'm working my way through college. In the past, I've had to get a job, work until I saved up enough money to attend a semester, then quit to go to school. When the money ran out, I'd get another job."

"Which does not solve my problem. I want someone who will stay longer than a few months."

"But that's the wonderful thing about the position you're offering. I can go to school at the same time I work if you'll agree to letting your daughters spend a few hours a week in a great child-care facility at ODU. It's set up for students to drop kids off while we're in class. I thought that would be acceptable. It'd just be an hour or two a day, four days a week, and would give your girls structured playtime with other children."

"ODU?"

"Old Dominion University right here in Norfolk. With the job you're offering, I wouldn't have to quit to attend another semester of school. I can attend classes and still watch your daughters. And I can assure you the child-care facility at the university is top-notch."

She'd thought it through. It'd mean so much to her to keep going, not have to take time off to earn enough money for the next semester. If only he didn't object. She'd be perfect for his children and the job would be perfect for her."

He studied her through dispassionate eyes. His expression didn't give a hint of his thoughts.

"What are you studying?" he asked.

"Graphic arts. I would study fine art, but there aren't a lot of career opportunities unless an artist is really super. I'm good, but not super. But I can combine my love for color, lines, shapes, and texture in graphics and enjoy doing it almost as much. That field definitely offers more career opportunities once I get my degree and some more experience. And for recreation, I still paint and sketch and work with pastels. So I indulge myself with both the practical side and the purely creative."

Arden swallowed and smiled brightly. This wasn't going as easily as she'd hoped. When he said nothing, she began again. She *couldn't* lose this opportunity.

"As for experience, I know lots about kids."

Raising her hand, she touched her index finger.

"First, from working at the restaurant, I know how children should and shouldn't behave in public. What they like to eat and how to keep them entertained when they're bored. Second," she touched the next finger, "from working at the beach, I've seen lots of kids and understand safety rules and how to enforce them. I know CPR. I have a certificate in first aid."

She smiled smugly. He'd probably appreciate that.

"And third," she touched another finger, "working at the day-care center gave me hands-on experience. The ages ranged from two to six."

He said nothing, just watched as she talked.

Taking another breath, Arden continued.

"At the library, I was the one to read for the children's hour. So I know what kinds of books kids like, especially young ones. I believe your girls are five and three?"

He nodded, but remained silent.

Not used to so little feedback, Arden wondered if he was merely biding his time until she stopped talking to tell her the job was not for her. Or was he truly listening? What else could she add?

"Merry Maid was a housecleaning service, so I can teach them proper techniques to keep their rooms tidy," she finished with triumph.

"I don't want to hire a nanny only to have her leave in a few months when something better comes along," he said slowly. "The girls' mother is dead. They've already had to go through one bout of separation and grief. My sister has been watching them and now she's leaving. Another bout of separation. I don't want a third soon."

He stood and picked up the folder.

"I'm looking for an older woman who would offer stability and reliability. And who won't go off with no notice the first time something goes wrong, or some man comes along and sweeps her off her feet."

"Older women can be swept off their feet, too," she countered swiftly. "And I don't plan to get married, so there's no worry there. Not that I'm the type to get swept off my feet. I'm determined to get my degree, to find work in my field and make a name for myself. Ever since high school, that's been my driving ambition."

He raised an eyebrow.

"Yet, you're trying to hire on to do something that has nothing to do with your chosen career. You'd do better to get an internship with a graphic arts place or ad agency. I expect meals to be on time, a certain amount of care around the house, though I have a cleaning service that does the major work. And a lot of attention paid to my children."

"I can do it."

"There's more to this job than just watching the girls. There are trips to the doctors and dentist. Shopping when they need new clothes."

"If I can work and attend classes, I'll graduate in another three semesters. I'd be willing to give you another six months after that. By then your younger daughter will be in kindergarten and you'll have after-school care available for both."

"That isn't enough."

"Why not?"

Arden thought she was being generous in agreeing to stay. It'd put her future on hold, but she'd relish the chance to finish school sooner. Why couldn't he see she offered the perfect solution?

She really wanted this job, no *needed* it. Otherwise, who knew how long it'd be before she'd graduate? She was already twenty-five. If she could be lucky enough to combine work and college, she'd be twenty-seven by the time she graduated. She wasn't getting any younger.

"My job is such that I can be gone with an hour's notice and I may not return home for several days, sometimes longer. I need someone responsible to be there twenty-four hours a day, seven days a week, to take care of my children when I'm gone. Someone they'll know and trust. Someone I know and trust and can depend on."

"I'm dependable *and* reliable. And I'm willing to negotiate almost anything."

Arden didn't want to appear desperate, but she was. She had no apartment, no current job, and finals started next month. She needed to get settled before then. Why couldn't he cooperate?

"It doesn't appear that you have much trouble finding

work. Seven jobs in seven years," he said.

"But I had a place to stay that cost nothing. Now I don't. That means it'll take me that much longer to save enough to pay for a full semester. And the workload at school is always so heavy, I can't work most jobs and keep up with my assignments. But I could manage with your girls. I can do my projects at night while they sleep. I'd be the best nanny you'll ever find."

"What happened to your home?"

She took a deep breath. It wasn't really any of his business. Especially if the interview was the sole contact she had with the man. And she really didn't want to go into it all. It always made her furious.

"Circumstances changed, that's all. One aspect that appealed strongly to me about your position is that I'd have room and board. I'd be great with your kids. Call the librarian, she'll verify how much the story hours were loved. Attendance increased by leaps and bounds while I was there. Call the day-care center, they'll tell you how reliable I am. Call any of the people on the list you want. They'll all tell you I'm conscientious, trustworthy. I never miss work. I'm never late. And I work hard, giving a full day's worth for a day's pay."

Brendan Ferguson almost smiled at her impassioned speech. She really seemed to want the job. He glanced back at the folder, knowing the prudent thing would be to keep searching. Despite her enthusiasm, her listing of accomplishments that would enable her to watch Hailey and Avery, he didn't want Arden Glover.

He wanted someone older, more settled.

Someone who wasn't pretty, vivacious, and so alive.

Startled at his train of thought, he kept his eyes on the folder. He'd learned to analyze things quickly and decide with little to go on but his gut instinct. But the feelings crowding him now had nothing to do with a nanny for his daughters.

Maybe a younger woman would be better able to keep up with the girls. Not that they were a problem. Still, at five and three, they had a lot of energy. Yet because they were so young, he didn't want their lives disrupted again anytime soon.

He had to admit that none of the other women he'd interviewed met all his requirements. Not that there'd been that many applicants. Only seven before Arden Glover.

Time was growing short. His sister, Ella, was leaving next week and he had to find someone before her departure.

He looked at Arden. She met his gaze squarely. Her blue eyes shone with sincerity. So different from the caramel brown of Lannie's eyes.

Of course, everything about Arden Glover was as different from his late wife as possible to be. Lannie had been petite, sweet, shy, and sexy in a quiet, womanly way. She hadn't wanted a career. She'd loved caring for their home, watching Hailey. She'd so been looking forward to the birth of their second child.

Her dark brown hair and brown eyes had passed to their daughters. At least he had that part of her forever.

But he missed her with an ache that never quite went away, even after three years.

Time was running out. If he didn't find someone to watch the girls by the time Ella left, he didn't know what he'd do.

"Avery starts first grade in three years. I'd want a commitment for that long," he said at last, his mind searching for alternatives.

"Three years?" Arden repeated, dismayed. That would make another delay to starting her career.

Her eyes glazed over a bit as if she were looking a long way into the future. Brendan watched as he could almost see how her mind was working. Either way, she decided, he'd have to live with it. Three years or goodbye.

And if she refused the terms, he'd have to continue trying to find someone before Ella left.

When she looked at him again, Brendan almost imagined he could see her resolve strengthen.

"I agree. Three years it is. As long as I can take your daughters to child-care while I'm in class. And I have a bunch of paraphernalia for art. I need to bring that, too. Will there be room?"

He nodded once. "My sister's been watching the girls since their mother died. But she recently married and she and her husband are leaving next Saturday. He's in the navy and been posted to San Diego. I'd need you settled in before then, preferably as soon as possible. Is that a problem?"

"Nope," she said breezily.

"When I'm home, you have weekends free. But if I'm away, I need to know you are there with the girls all the time."

"No problem. I understand."

Something about this arrangement still worried him. Was she too young? Would she really devote her attention to the children?

Her entire attitude annoyed him. She was too casual, carefree.

He wished he could judge how sincere she was in stating she wasn't interested in marriage. Someone that pretty must have men lined up. Maybe she hadn't met the right one yet. Did she date a lot?

Brendan shook his head, shoving the unsettling feeling aside. He was hiring a woman to watch his daughters, nothing more. What she did in her spare time was her own business. He'd have his secretary call her past employers to learn what she could about Arden Glover. But unless something turned up, which he did not expect, he was sincere in his offer of employment.

"So, how soon can you move in?"

"My things are already in boxes, so I can load up and bring them to your place as soon as you give me directions. I can be there today if you like or tomorrow."

"I'll do some checking of your references today and if everything's okay, I'll call tonight to give you directions. Can you start tomorrow afternoon?" he said slowly, wondering why her things were in boxes.

"Sure, no problem. Thanks a bunch. I'll take great care of your girls. I'm used to watching others, you know. Until a few weeks ago, I lived with my great-aunts and have taken care of them for the last few years. They recently moved to a retirement home over near Ocean View. They always loved the beach and when they had to move, they chose to live near the water. Of course, the place has some stupid rules."

She stopped abruptly.

Brendan waited a moment, unexpectedly curious about the stupid rules. And even more curious about this woman than he wanted to admit.

Arden rose and stepped closer to hold out her hand.

"I'll look forward to your call."

He shook her hand briefly, an instant awareness catching him by surprise. She was tall, slender, but with curves in all the right places. Her vest flowed over full breasts, a hint of a shadow at the Vee of the brocade. With her this close, he could smell her scent, light and fragrant, like a summer flower.

"I don't know what to call you," she said breathlessly, tugging to pull her hand free. "Mr. Ferguson?"

Surprised to realize he still held her hand, he released it instantly.

"Brendan will do," he said, reaching for the folder. "The girls and I will call you Arden."

"Good. That's what my friends call me," she said with a smile.

He looked at her. He didn't plan on becoming friends. Theirs was strictly a business arrangement.

But he said, "I have your phone number. I'll call you later."

"I look forward to meeting the children tomorrow."

With another bright smile, she walked out the door, her stride limber and energetic.

Brendan leaned back against the table, listening to her footsteps as she headed for the elevators. She was nothing like what he'd pictured as a nanny for his children.

But since he'd interviewed no one who matched his vague image of a widowed, gray-haired, plump woman who loved to bake and adored children, he suspected his vision was impossible. Arden was the best he could come up with on such short notice. He hoped he wasn't making a mistake.

For a moment, the memory of her swaying hips as she walked away lingered. He wondered what her hair would look like released from the clasp that held it back. Wavy at least, curly, maybe. It was long enough to brush her shoulder blades. He'd like to see it swirling around her face.

Scowling at that unwarranted thought, he picked up the folder. He needed to get back to work.

He caught sight of her standing by the elevator as he headed for his office and slowed his pace. He bet she rarely wore a skirt. Something about the way she moved made him think of shorts or jeans which would display those long legs to advantage.

He did his best to ignore her as she stepped into the elevator. Lannie had been dead three years, and he'd never even looked at another woman in all that time.

He certainly would not become personally interested in a temporary nanny for his children, no matter how feminine and appealing and sexy she was.

Chapter Two

Brendan stayed home the next afternoon. He'd had his secretary rearrange his schedule so he could be there with his daughters when Arden Glover arrived.

He'd called Arden last night to confirm her references had checked out perfectly and to request she come around one o'clock, just after lunch. That way, he reasoned, she could get settled and spend time with the girls while his sister, Ella, prepared dinner. If they all hit it off, maybe Ella could leave earlier than originally planned to finish her own packing.

Brendan stood in front of the picture window of the home he'd bought after Lannie's death. The yard was pristine, the grass cut into a uniform two inches. The shrubbery by the house was neatly trimmed below the window. The flower gardens in two symmetrical plots were weeded. Their colorful blossoms livened the deep green of the grass.

It had been impossible to remain in the house they' shared after his wife's death. But sometimes he felt it had been harder to leave. At least there he'd been in a place she'd known. She'd never seen this house. The difference made the break seem even more final.

Not that it got more final than death.

When a dusty old station wagon turned into his driveway, he studied it curiously. Someone turning around, no doubt. But when it stopped and the driver's door flew open, he looked more closely.

Two seconds later, Arden Glover climbed out.

He'd been right about the long, sexy legs. Encased in stretch pants, they seemed to go on forever. The sleeveless tunic hit her mid-thigh, but when she leaned back in the car, the tunic rode up, revealing a taut, rounded bottom.

Brendan was used to making snap decisions for corporate accounts worth millions of dollars. He was known for his acumen and ability to cut through any problem and find a solution. His new nanny hadn't even walked through the front door, and Brendan suddenly became convinced that he'd made a huge mistake.

And it was entirely personal. There was something about Arden Glover that made him aware that he was a man and she was a very attractive woman.

Too late to do anything about it today. She was here and ready to start work. But one look at her and he knew he needed to continue to search for a more suitable nanny. One he wouldn't mind sharing a house with for years on end. A woman who didn't remind him he was still fairly young, and had his whole life ahead of him. One who didn't prompt feelings of loneliness and awareness.

Resolutely heading for the front door, he called up the stairs to the girls. He'd get Arden settled, then stay out of her way.

"Your directions were great," Arden said when she spotted him.

She'd already taken a large box from the back of the car and was balancing it with one hand against the dusty side.

Eyeing the ancient vehicle with some trepidation, Brendan joined her at the rear. He took the box from her, surprised at the heaviness.

"Oh, thanks. I wanted to carry something in when I went. We can unload everything later, but I thought why waste a trip inside empty-handed? Now that I'm staying and all."

She took another box out of the car.

"I'm glad my previous employers all gave me a good reference or I know I wouldn't be here now. Mrs. McFanney at the flower shop told me you sounded very stern. But I assured her I was here to watch your girls, not you."

She laughed, and Brendan felt an odd quickening of his breath. She chatted nonstop as he led the way into the house, commenting on the pretty houses and the mature trees in the neighborhood. Her observations had him looking at his neighbors' homes in a new light.

Exclaiming over the flowers in the garden, telling him how excited she was to be moving in, she seemed to go on forever. Did she ever stop for breath?

Pausing just inside the door, she did just that—stopped talking as she turned around, gazing at everything.

He wondered how long the silence would last before she rushed into speech again. He wasn't used to such chattiness and considered timing this brief pause.

The house was nothing extraordinary, certainly not enough to leave her speechless. Two stories, with five bedrooms, four upstairs and one off the family room. He'd been specific with the bedrooms, knowing he'd eventually need live-in help.

"This is great. Light and airy."

She dumped her box and walked into the living room with a suppleness that he enjoyed watching. Did she dance he wondered, as he placed the box he carried beside hers and followed her into the room. She moved as if she did, lithely and gracefully.

"Hi, I'm Arden," she said, crossing to the wide sofa where two little girls sat side by side. Sinking onto the floor in front of them, she drew two small books from her voluminous shoulder bag.

"I brought you each a present to celebrate our first day together."

She smiled and held out one book to the younger of the girls, whose brown hair was contained in two curly ponytails on either side of her head.

"This is a favorite of mine. Do you already have it? *Green Eggs and Ham*."

She waited while the little girl looked at the book and then at her father.

Brendan nodded, surprised. He hadn't expected Arden to bring the girls anything. He was oddly touched she'd thought of it.

"And this one is for you. It's another favorite, *Go, Dog, Go.* Maybe we can have a big dog party one day."

Arden held out the book to the older child. Her glossy brown hair hung down her back like silk. Pulled back from her face, it moved when she ducked her head bashfully.

Brendan nodded to Hailey, and she took the book, a shy smile for Arden.

"Thank you," she said. "We don't have a dog. How can we have a dog party?"

"We'll have to work on that," Arden said, smiling at the child.

Avery clutched her book to her chest, but hadn't said a word.

"Avery, say thank you," Brendan prompted.

"Thank you."

Her voice was quiet. She was the child who reminded him the most of Lannie. He wished her mother had known her, had seen how precious she was. But Lannie had died giving birth to Avery.

"Arden, Hailey is five, and Avery is three. Say hi to Arden, girls. She's come to take care of you," Brendan said, squatting near Avery.

He felt his heart swell with love for his daughters.

"Are you our new mommy?" Hailey asked.

Arden shook her head. A pang blasted through her at the words, and she had to work to keep her smile in place. She'd never be anyone's mommy.

"No, honey, I'm not," she said gently. "I'm your new babysitter. I'm going to watch you and your sister when your daddy's not home. We'll have lots of fun together. What's your favorite game?"

Arden tried to concentrate on the girls and ignore the male hunk beside her. He wasn't wearing a suit today. Instead, the jeans that molded his legs looked old, worn and fit as if he'd been poured into them and certainly delineated the powerful muscles of his thighs better than the trousers had yesterday.

But it was what was revealed by the white T-shirt with the sleeves ripped out that had her catching her breath. The smooth skin of his upper arms moved as the muscles expanded and contracted. She longed to run her fingertips over those muscles, feel the heat and the strength. The very thought had her stomach in knots and her brain finding it difficult to think clearly.

She was here to watch his daughters, for heaven's sake,

not fantasize about their father.

Fantasize? No, it was an appreciation for an excellent example of human anatomy, that's all.

Yeah, right.

"I thought I heard voices."

Arden glanced over her shoulder to see a tall, striking woman enter the room. She had the same dark-colored hair as Brendan Ferguson and looked a bit like him around the mouth, but her eyes were a lighter gray and friendly.

"You must be Arden Glover. I'm Ella Robinson, Brendan's sister. And I'm so glad you've come. We were running out of time. My husband swore we were leaving next Saturday no matter what, but I know he secretly thought I'd end up staying here until Brendan found someone."

Arden scrambled to her feet and shook hands with Ella.

"Now you can leave without worrying. I'll take great care of them. I understand you're moving to San Diego?" she said.

"That's right, clear across the country," Ella said in a friendly tone. "Ever been there?"

"No. I was born here in Norfolk and I've never been anywhere outside of Virginia, except for a school trip to DC."

"We're from here, too, originally. But our father is Navy. I take it Brendan told you I married a career naval officer. I expect I'll see a lot more of the world during the next couple of decades. My lot in life, I guess, constantly changing duty stations. I'm glad you didn't have to give notice elsewhere so you could start right away. Brendan could have found day care somewhere close, but there's always the chance he'll be called away in the middle of the night."

Brendan rose and headed for the archway.

"I'll unload your things. Ella can show you your room and go over the schedule with you."

Arden nodded, following Ella as she wound through the house to a spacious bedroom off the family room.

The two girls tagged along, each carrying her new book.

"This is it. Bathroom's over there," Ella said as she stopped in the center of the large room. "It's separate from the rest of the bedrooms, so you'll have some privacy. Brendan has a baby monitor in the girls' room. When he's not home, you can take the speaker and listen for them from down here."

Arden nodded, dropping her shoulder bag on the bed and gazing around at what would be her room for the next three years. Windows lined one wall, overlooking a huge backyard where tall elms and poplars provided shade from the hot Virginia sunshine. There were no paintings on the walls, she noted, but she had plenty she could put up to feel at home.

Studying the furniture, Arden liked the light oak, and even though the bed was queen-size, there was plenty of open space in the room. Enough for her easel and paints. The windows would give her plenty of natural light.

For a moment she felt a regret for losing her old room.

She missed the huge old maple tree that brushed against the house in the wind. Missed the flowers Aunt Love had so patiently tended. Missed the floorboards that creaked comfortably underfoot whenever she walked.

But it was gone, and there was nothing to be done about it. This was much better than the tiny bedroom she'd been using in Patti's small apartment.

"Come on in," she said to the girls who hovered in the doorway. "You can help me unpack and tell me all about what you like to do, which are your favorite games, and maybe tell me a story."

By dinnertime, Arden knew the job would not be quite as she'd envisioned it with her optimistic imagination. The children were wonderfully behaved–maybe too good. Ella had gone over their schedule in great detail. Everything seemed outlined down to an exact science what time they got up, when they played, when they napped, when they bathed. Even meals were at specific times each day.

"Brendan doesn't always get to eat with them," Ella said when the girls had gone upstairs to play and she and Arden had moved to the kitchen to prepare dinner.

"Since they eat right at six each evening, if he's delayed at the office, he gets something to eat before he comes home. He's good about getting here before they go to bed. Of course, if he's out on an assignment..." she trailed off and looked at Arden. "You realize he can be called away at a moment's notice? If there's a problem in Latin America or something, he's often called in for hostage negotiations. Or if threats have been made and clients want instant security measures installed. Sometimes he goes, other times he delegates the assignment to one of the people who works for him. We never know when he'll be called. That's the price he pays for being one of the best in his field."

Arden nodded, wondering how she could tactfully question the girls' schedule. It seemed too rigid for young children. Structure was important, but flexibility had its place, too.

"You've written everything," Arden said slowly. "Did Brendan tell you I'd be taking classes at ODU? I'll put the girls in child care there when I'm attending class."

"No, he didn't mention it."

Ella frowned and gazed out the kitchen window for a moment, tapping one finger against the counter.

"I guess he knows what he's doing," she said at last. Turning to face Arden, she continued, "You'll be going to class at the same time each day, so that'll be fine. Brendan runs a tight ship, and he thinks routine is important for children."

"This is a ship?"

Ella laughed softly.

"No, sorry, that's just an expression our father always uses. He's an admiral. The entire time we were growing up, he made sure Mom kept our household on strict schedules. I guess Brendan picked it up from Dad. Anyway, with routines established, things run more smoothly. Making up for when they don't, I suppose."

"How did the girls' mother die?" Arden asked bluntly, knowing it'd be far easier to question Ella than her formidable brother.

Ella looked surprised, then glanced toward the empty doorway as if to see if Brendan was there.

"We don't talk about Lannie. Brendan hasn't gotten over losing her. She had an embolism and died unexpectedly delivering Avery."

"That was three years ago?" Arden asked.

She'd worked in a hospice for a while, and understood the stages of grief and recovery. Three years seemed like a long time to avoid talking about a loved one who had died. Not that there was any set length of time. Each person had to heal in his or her own way. But still Ella nodded. "She never even got to hold Avery. It really shook us all up. She was so young."

"That's sad. I'm sorry for your loss and the girls'. It's tough not having your mother when you're growing up. I know because mine died when I was seven. I guess I just didn't notice pictures of Lannie in the girls' room when you gave me the house tour."

"There aren't any. Brendan couldn't stand to be reminded at first. He was so crazy about her. I guess we never thought later to put any out. I know he has lots of photos somewhere unless he destroyed them after she died. He was devastated. They were the perfect couple, and he adored Lannie."

Lannie was a pretty name. Had his wife been pretty? Arden wondered. For a moment she envied the woman. She'd never have a perfect marriage. In fact, she didn't plan to marry at all. But it didn't stop her from wondering what it'd be like to be adored.

At least he has his daughters.

"What are their favorite foods?" Arden asked, trying to ignore her curiosity about Brendan Ferguson's wife. Or her new employer. She was here to care for his children, nothing more.

Arden considered all Ella had told her when they sat down to eat promptly at six o'clock. She watched Hailey and Avery, pleased to note their table manners were superb. Nothing like some children she'd seen in the restaurant. These young ladies were quiet and well behaved.

Maybe *too* quiet.

"Did you tell your daddy we read the new books?" she asked when there was a lull in the adult conversation.

Brendan looked at her, then at the girls.

"Arden read us the new books, Daddy," Hailey said.

"That was nice. Did you enjoy them?" Brendan asked.

She nodded.

Avery looked at her sister, then nodded.

Arden waited for Brendan to ask them what the books

were about, or where they'd been read, or something to continue the dialogue. But he resumed eating, saying nothing.

Arden glared at him.

He looked back at her, narrowing his eyes at her expression. "Something wrong?"

She sighed and shook her head. If he didn't know, it wasn't her place to tell him tonight.

She continued to observe the interaction between the family members. She had little to go by; her aging great-aunts were the only living relatives she had. And they had all talked at mealtimes, sharing their days.

She missed living with them.

Feeling very homesick for a house that no longer was hers, she finished her meal, looking forward to slipping off to her room for the night. This was only the first day. There'd be time enough to think things through and make any changes she felt necessary in the weeks to come.

By late afternoon the next day, Ella had left to finish packing her own household to prepare for moving. Brendan had departed for his office. And Arden had spent the day alone with two little girls.

Delighted to discover they were not the perfect little angels she'd thought yesterday, Arden chased after them all day. Playing ball in the backyard had been a hit. So had hide-and-seek.

After a lunch of peanut butter and banana sandwiches,

which they had never tried before and declared a new favorite, they'd settled in the queen-size bed in Arden's room and she read the new books again. Both girls had dropped off quickly, giving Arden time to tidy their room and have a quiet moment sipping a glass of iced tea.

Now they played on the kitchen floor while she prepared dinner. Contrary to Ella's assessment that they liked pretty much everything, the girls had favorites. Hailey loved spaghetti and meatballs, and Avery loved pork chops.

Since she was unsure whether or not Brendan would be home for dinner, she elected to make spaghetti. It was easy to stretch or to cook just enough for the three of them.

The girls played pickup sticks with a few uncooked noodles. Every so often, one would break, and Arden would toss a whole one to them. She'd sweep the mess up in a second when they were finished.

They were thrilled with the new game, and their laughter was a delight to hear as she stirred the sauce.

"How did things go today?" Brendan asked, standing in the doorway to the kitchen.

Arden spun around and felt her heart skip a beat. He looked as potent as ever. There was definitely a lot to be said for an exquisitely tailored business suit that revealed wide shoulders and cried to be taken off.

Stop it, she admonished herself, banishing fantasies until she was alone and could give free rein to them. She had a job to do.

"Hi."

Was that breathless voice hers? She cleared her throat and took a deep breath.

"I wasn't sure if you'd be home for supper or not. It won't be much longer. Avery, Hailey, go give your daddy a hug and a kiss. He can tell you all about his day while I finish making dinner. And you can tell him all we did."

Brendan looked at the pan on the stove, frowning. "Isn't dinner ready yet? It's almost six."

Arden waved her hand around vaguely.

"Actually, it's almost ready. Another ten minutes or so. And I doubt anyone will perish if dinner isn't on the table precisely at six. Do you help set the table, or are the girls supposed to do that?"

"I thought you would. Isn't that woman's work?"

Arden froze. Her eyes locked with his, and she felt a stirring of complete disbelief. Her temper simmered. Before she could remember her great-aunt's admonition to count to ten before giving in to her anger, she spoke.

"Excuse me? Did you say it's *woman's* work?"

Brendan hesitated and then nodded slowly, his attention focused completely on her.

"I don't believe you said that."

Slamming the spoon down on the counter, Arden dusted her hands together.

"I can't believe it. I won't believe it."

"What?"

"That anyone in this day and age would even *think* something like that, much less *say* it. *Woman's work?* What a sexist remark. If that's the way you feel, I need to reconsider this position."

"What's to reconsider? You signed on for three years. Quitting is not an option. You just started."

Was there a hint of panic in his voice?

"I did not know I'd be working for a, a, a Neanderthal. Thinking like yours went out during World War Two when women went to work to keep America going while men went off to fight. If you think for one second I could continue working for anyone who thinks like that, you're nuts. Obviously, you misled me in the interview."

"Whoa, time out."

He stepped closer, crunching his way through dried spaghetti noodles. Frowning, he walked around his daughters until he was close to Arden.

"I meant nothing by it. I thought–"

"Ha. That makes it even worse. You just say things like that and not mean them?"

Brendan shook his head, rubbing his hand over his face. Looking at her again, he took a deep breath, obviously controlling himself.

"Let's start over. I thought you'd set the table based on

the fact Ella did every time. If you want me to, I will."

"And who did it before that?" she asked, hands on her hips.

He hesitated a moment and glanced at the girls who were ignoring the exchange, busy playing their new game.

He met her eyes again.

"When the girls' mother was alive, she always did. Lannie said a man had enough to do with bringing home the bacon. She enjoyed taking care of the house. It was all she ever wanted."

Arden's indignation died instantly at the bleak tone in his voice. It sounded to her like the women in Brendan's life had spoiled him rotten. But she hadn't been hired to be a maid. Just to watch the girls and take care of them. And teach them.

One thing she'd be sure to teach them was they were not on this earth to wait on men.

Unless, of course, they wanted to. Like his Lannie apparently had. And his sister.

"Well."

She didn't know what to say. Her temper was quick to flare, but never stayed hot for long.

"If setting the table becomes an issue, I'll do it when I'm home. But you can't quit." The steel in his voice warned her not to push her luck.

"Okay."

Clearing her throat, Arden tried to smile. "Sometimes I

get a bit hot-headed and blurt out things I don't always mean. Not that I didn't mean that about not working for a Neanderthal because I did, but maybe there are extenuating circumstances here."

"Run that by me again?" Brendan said, looking perplexed.

She laughed nervously and shook her head. Picking up the spoon, she stirred the sauce once more, checked on the noodles and glanced at the oven. The savory aroma of hot garlic bread filled the room. She prayed the heat in her cheeks didn't show.

"Never mind. It's not important, except I'm sorry I jumped to conclusions. Dinner is ready," she said quickly.

In the end, everyone picked up forks and plates in the kitchen and each carried their own to the table.

Wondering what other pitfalls lay ahead, Arden waited until the children began to eat before looking at Brendan from beneath her lashes. She couldn't react so impetuously every time something came up. She needed this job. He paid her salary. He had the right to dictate the rules of his household.

And she had signed on for three years.

"Maybe we should get together tonight after the children are in bed and go over some ground rules. Ella reviewed their schedule with me, but I have some questions and suggestions. And obviously I need to learn a bit more about you and how your family operates before I make another gaff like earlier," she said in what she thought was a reasonable tone.

He nodded. "Fine. As soon as you get the girls in bed, come back down and we'll talk."

"Aren't you going to tuck them in, or is this another aspect of woman's work? Exactly what do you do with these kids, Mr. Ferguson?"

Chapter Three

Brendan looked at Arden, feeling the condemnation in her gaze. Who was she to pass judgment on the way he ran his household? She had only moved in yesterday. *She* worked for *him*. It was up to her to accommodate herself to his schedule, not for him to change his ways.

"Lannie took care of child raising. She said that was her job, just as I have mine. Besides, if I start routines, then disrupt them because of being called away, it's more unsettling for the girls."

"Kids are resilient, they can adapt."

"The way we have things set up works for us," he said with finality.

If he'd spoken to one of the men at work in that tone, they'd have immediately complied, not talked back.

"Maybe it works, but it doesn't sound real joyful," she muttered.

Brendan refrained from making a reply. Arden was nothing like his wife. Lannie had been the first to suggest his unscheduled departures could disrupt young lives. Nothing had changed when Ella took over. He still made trips, worked late, and couldn't count on being home at the same time every day.

Ironically, Lannie had been the one to die. His job was occasionally dangerous, there was no denying that. But instead of his leaving her a widow, Lannie had left him. And with their two little girls.

He missed the soothing routines she'd established. Her arms greeting him. He missed her.

Now, instead of her warm smile opposite him at the table, he had a stranger glaring at him.

"What?" he asked.

Had he missed something?

"Hailey asked if you liked spaghetti. It's her favorite dinner," Arden said. Her voice was calm, but fire flashed in her eyes.

"It is?" He looked at Hailey and smiled. "I love spaghetti, sweetheart. It was my favorite meal when I was a kid."

"Arden let me help," she said proudly.

"Good for Arden."

His gaze met hers across the table and he nodded once. At least the girls seem to like her, and the first day was always difficult. Things would work out. They'd discuss the children and get things settled tonight. He would make this arrangement work. What choice did he have?

Some time later, Arden slipped from the girls' bedroom

and headed down the stairs. Brendan had come up to tuck them in, after all, and she wanted to give him this private time with his daughters. They were freshly scrubbed and looked adorable in matching nightgowns. The contrast between the small, feminine little girls and their rugged daddy tugged at her heart. She'd love to paint the three of them.

Maybe in that scenario, Brendan would be a warrior at rest, with adoring children at his side. In a garden, with his honed masculine body in stark contrast to the gentle flowers and serene setting.

She sat in a chair in the living room, truly relaxing for the first time that day. She missed her aunts. Maybe she'd run out tomorrow and see them. And take the girls. They'd love Eugenia and Love. She'd have to ask Brendan if she could have her aunts visit when he was gone. Aunt Love missed her kitchen, and Arden knew no one could resist her aunt's baking. The girls would find it a special treat to bake cookies with her. Arden always had.

"What did you do with them today? They're so tired, I think they were asleep before I closed their door. Didn't they nap?" Brendan asked as he walked into the living room.

Marched in, more like it, Arden thought, sitting up and going on alert. Her fatigue fled. Suddenly, she felt more alive than ever.

"Of course, they took naps, but they had a busy day. We played in the yard this morning. Hide-and-seek is still lots of fun for them and with all the shrubbery and lawn furniture in the back, we had lots of places to hide."

Brendan sat on the sofa, stretched out his long legs and leaned his head back, closing his eyes

"Hide-and-seek wore them out?"

"No. We also went for a walk to explore the neighborhood. I was hoping to find a park within walking distance so we could have a change of scenery from time to time, but we didn't find one."

Arden stopped and looked at him.

"Am I keeping you up? We could talk tomorrow if you'd rather."

He opened one eye, shook his head, and closed it again.

"I'm not tired, I'm listening to you. I can concentrate better with my eyes shut. So no nearby park."

"No, but it was a long walk. Then we had lunch and I read their new books while they lay on my bed. That's when they fell asleep and slept for a couple of hours. After they woke up, we played ball in the backyard until I started dinner. I can get you some coffee or something. I didn't bake today, but will once I get to the store and buy the ingredients. You have little in the cupboards."

Brendan raised his head and opened his eyes.

"Did Ella show you where I keep the money for household expenses? Cash for groceries. I usually write checks for the bills. We need to get an account for you to sign on for the times when I'm gone."

His gaze drifted down to her legs.

Arden shifted uneasily. Maybe she should have taken time to put on her stretch pants or a skirt. But the shorts were comfortable in the Virginia heat. The house was cooler now, but during the day, she'd left the windows open for the fresh air. It wasn't yet full summer when it'd be too hot to ignore the air-conditioning.

Brendan's gray eyes locked on hers.

"I'll take a long lunch hour tomorrow and we'll meet at the bank. Now about those ground rules you wanted to discuss," Brendan said.

"It's a matter of philosophy, I guess," Arden said slowly. "You threw me for a loop with your comment about woman's work tonight."

"And hit a hot button."

She nodded. "I was raised by two aunts who did everything at home, so I guess I believe everyone should pitch in. If you have different ideas, maybe we need to discuss them. If I can't fit in, we should discover this before the girls become attached to me."

Brendan nodded.

"Their mother and my own were full-time homemakers."

He looked away, his voice softening when he spoke again.

"Lannie loved being a wife and then a mother. She fixed up our house to suit her, and it was always immaculate. Her meals were creative and elegant. Once Hailey was born, she sewed little dresses for her, made the curtains in the nursery. We each had our roles in the marriage and she enjoyed being a homemaker. I guess I still expect the same thing, which is unfair to you."

Arden stared at him. It was the most she'd ever heard him say. And so eloquently. His love for his dead wife shone in every word. She needed to cut him some slack. His entire world changed with the death of his wife.

What would it be like to be loved like that? To know she was the bright spot in someone's life? To know that even years later, her loss would be catastrophic.

"But that role is not necessarily the right one for everyone. Wouldn't you want your daughters to grow up knowing they have a choice for what they want or don't want to do?" she said quietly, trying to keep her mind focused on the present, and not off dreaming about what couldn't be.

"Of course I want that for them. But setting or not setting the table won't warp them for life."

"No, but hearing a man say it's woman's work might. While I'm here, I plan to teach them how to clean and put things away. Everyone needs to know basic housekeeping to keep their own place neat, not just girls."

"Your point is made. And taken. I'll refrain from chauvinistic Neanderthal comments in the future, if you'll refrain from making my daughters ardent feminists."

Arden smiled, happy to discover Brendan Ferguson had a sense of humor.

"Deal. Besides, when they're older, you might be glad they can mow the lawn or change the oil in your car."

"And you can teach them that?"

"Not at this young age. But yeah, pretty much anything."

"Undoubtedly the result of your aunts' teaching."

"That's right. We did everything around that old house and cared for the cars to save a few dollars," Arden said in fond remembrance.

"The same aunts who now live at Ocean View?"

She nodded. "I really miss them."

"Then why are you here and they there?"

"It's a long story."

Brendan felt a sense of anticipation. She couldn't possibly explain what happened in just a few words, he thought. He settled back against the cushions to listen to her. He liked her voice, low and tinged with a hint of a Virginia accent.

"I've got a few minutes," he murmured.

"Then I'd rather talk about the girls and give you my life's history another time," she said with some asperity.

He looked over at her lazily.

"It's eight forty-five at night. You don't look old enough to have a long history behind you. Tell me more about yourself and then we'll discuss the girls."

Arden sighed theatrically and shrugged. "My folks died

when I was seven and I went to live with Aunt Eugenia and Aunt Love."

"Love?"

"Her name is really Pearl Lovell Glover, but her parents called her Love as a child and it just stuck. Do you want Aunt Eugenia's full name, too?"

He shook his head, feeling a hint of amusement.

"Anyway, they're my dad's aunts actually, so are my great-aunts. They were in their early sixties when I went to live with them."

"They seem old to have the care of a seven-year-old," Brendan murmured.

"It didn't seem so. They have more energy than most people half their age. Anyway, there wasn't anyone else. So, for better or worse, we were stuck with each other, although I realized later they could have refused to have me and sent me to foster care. Not that they'd ever do such a thing. They loved me right from the first. I was slower to fall for them, because I really missed my parents. But at least Aunt Eugenia and Aunt Love knew enough to give me time. Now, of course, I'm crazy about them, as is everyone else who knows them."

"Did you have a falling out?"

She glanced at him and frowned.

"Since you aren't still living together."

"No, the house they lived in for the last twenty-eight years didn't belong to them. They rented from Mr. Phelps. He was a character, too. Old as the hills when I first moved there. Anyway, it leaked when it rained, let the wind whistle through some rooms because the windows didn't close properly and cost a fortune to heat, but it was home. And inexpensive. Mr. Phelps had given them a low rent when they first moved in and never raised it."

"Let me guess. Mr. Phelps is no longer with us and his heirs weren't quite so generous?" Brendan guessed dryly.

Arden nodded. "Exactly right. His son couldn't wait to raise the rent. Only we didn't have enough to pay the extra amount he was asking, and it'd have been really dumb to spend so much rent on a house that's falling apart. So the aunts decided to check out a retirement home. They can afford the one they chose and love being by the beach."

"But that move left you out in the cold."

Arden looked at him warily. Brendan almost laughed at the expression on her face. The story sounded like a soap opera. Couldn't she see the humor in it?

"I have a good friend who invited me to stay with her. But her husband comes home soon from his deployment and I know they want to be alone. Besides, this great job opened up and here I am."

"So your cryptic comment at the interview about taking care of others meant you cared for your aunts?"

"Somewhat. For the last few years, I cooked most of the meals, though Aunt Love is the world's greatest baker. She makes the most marvelous cakes and pies. And her cookies are melt-in-your-mouth good. Eugenia has never been much of a cook and she has arthritis now, which limits all she can do. But both are sharp as a tack mentally. Their memory is much better than mine. You'll love them."

"What?"

"Oops, I meant, I assume I can invite people over occasionally? They'll want to see where I'm living. And the girls will love them. That's what I meant. Your girls will love them. Sort of like having grandparents around."

"They have grandparents in California."

"I know, Ella said your parents retired there."

"And their mother's parents live in Georgia. And come to visit twice a year."

"Any aunts and uncles?"

"Two aunts, two uncles."

"Well, if Hailey and Avery are used to relatives being around, they won't mind a couple more."

Brendan didn't want them to share Arden's relatives. He didn't want her to make a place in his daughters' lives that would be hard to fill once she moved on. And despite her assertion about not wanting marriage, he didn't trust her to remain for the full three years. Wasn't that why he was going to continue to search for a nanny who would fully meet his requirements?

That was the only reason. Not the feelings she engendered

in him whenever she was near. He could handle that. It was to safeguard his daughters that he needed to find a replacement for Arden soon.

"Why did you say marriage wasn't for you?" he asked, suddenly needing to know.

Maybe she could tell him something that would convince him she meant what she said and hadn't just thrown out the words to make a favorable impression at the interview.

She shook her head.

"We're not close enough to share something that personal. You'll just have to trust me on this. I don't expect to ever marry."

Rising, Arden smiled politely, but Brendan saw the distance in her eyes, and felt as if a wall had been established between them. Interesting reaction to a simple question.

"I'll finish up in the kitchen and turn in. Tell me where the bank is located and I'll meet you there tomorrow."

Brendan rose, standing close enough to her he could have reached out a hand and touched her shoulder.

"Want help in the kitchen?"

The words startled him. He'd never offered to help Lannie, though he'd enjoyed sitting at the kitchen island and drinking coffee with her while she worked.

"No, thanks. The bank?"

Obviously, the time to talk had ended. And they hadn't even started on the children. Why had the question about why she didn't wish to marry caused such a reaction? Was she recovering from the loss of someone as he was?

He never planned to remarry so he could understand that reason. If so, why not just come right out and say so?

I don't ever expect to marry. The words echoed in Arden's mind as she cleaned the pots and pans that had been soaking and put them away. She'd been careful for years not to get so involved with a man she'd have to tell him she could never have children. An occasional date was fine, especially if the man enjoyed the same activities she did. But at the first hint of a growing seriousness, she backed away.

She was content with her life and the plans she'd made for the future. She'd spend her passion on her work and find delight in other aspects of life, just like Aunt Love had done. She wouldn't repine for what couldn't be.

And for three years, she'd be a part of this family without any involvement in her heart. She'd do her best with these precious children, and by the end of her stay, she'd have her degree and maybe some experience to jump start her career. The fact she'd be twenty-eight by then didn't bother her. With her entire life still ahead of her, it didn't matter how long the basic training took. As long as she kept focused.

She snapped off the lights and went to her room. The boxes Brendan had brought in yesterday were still stacked in the corner. Maybe tomorrow she'd get some unpacked. First thing she'd look for would be her pastels and pen and ink so she could begin drawing again.

Maybe even sketch her warrior.

Getting ready for bed, Arden kept her emotions at bay. But once she slid beneath the sheets and switched off the lamp, they rose and threatened to topple her.

The longing for a mate never dissipated. Despite her tight control of her thoughts, the yearning surfaced. She wanted to be loved for herself and share the love that filled her with someone special. To know there was one person in the world who would cherish her, love her, support her dreams, and offer solace when things in life didn't always work out the way she hoped.

Fear sometimes swamped her. Fear for the lonely future that she faced the endless years she'd be alone once her aunts died.

Tonight she pushed it away, concentrating instead on how she would sketch Brendan as a warrior king of old. Castle ruins in the background, she decided as sleep claimed her.

Chapter Four

"Are you sure you want to do this?" Arden asked Brendan late the next morning when the woman behind the desk at the bank left for a moment to get the proper forms.

Arden and the girls had met Brendan at the bank shortly before eleven. Once he discussed adding Arden as a signer on his account, the full reality of the situation struck her. He was putting all his assets in her hands, at least all the monetary ones.

His parents, he'd explained, had power of attorney. But he'd also make sure she had one for the full care of the girls when he was gone.

"I mean, being able to sign on this account means I have access to all your money. I thought we'd just set up a household account."

He leaned close, his breath brushing her cheeks as he spoke. Arden could see the faint lines radiating from his eyes. Her fingers clenched tightly to keep from reaching up to touch him. They were in a public place, for heaven's sake. And he was just talking. But the urge was strong. She swallowed hard and tried to concentrate.

"If I trust you with my children, why wouldn't I trust you with my money? I can always get more money."

She knew he had no worries about her absconding with funds. But it surprised her to realize the depth of his trust.

"Okay. And you have nothing to worry about. I would never take your money," she said earnestly.

Brendan nodded. "I know."

He sat back as the bank official rejoined them.

Arden drew a deep breath and tried to relax her jangled nerves. The man was driving her wild, and he hadn't a clue. Which was as it should be. She simply could not let herself find him fascinating and bewitching. Or have him suspect for one instance how he had her hormones raging.

Remember to focus, she admonished herself.

Signing the cards where indicated, Arden tried to distance herself from the proceedings. She was a signer on his account. When he was away, it'd be up to her to make sure the bills were paid on time, the groceries were bought; the girls had clothes and shoes. The responsibility seemed heavy—almost that of a wife. She hoped he wouldn't be going anywhere for a long time.

"How about lunch at McDonald's?" Brendan asked as they paused on the sidewalk outside the bank. He held Avery in his arms and smiled down at Hailey.

Arden, for the first time in her life, didn't feel too tall standing next to Brendan.

She smiled at Hailey's enthusiastic response and reached for the child's hand.

"Shall we go, then? Your daddy has to get back to work soon."

"You drove your station wagon?" he asked as she paused by the dusty old car. "I have a car in the garage. I thought Ella told you to use it."

"She did. But I prefer driving my own. It may be old, but the engine is in perfect condition. My aunts would never let me drive something that wasn't totally safe."

"And who tuned it up last, you or them?"

Arden opened the back door and waited while Hailey scrambled inside.

"I did the last time, under Aunt Eugenia's close supervision. It runs like a top. Come on and be daring. I'll drive to Micky D's and you can see for yourself. Another advantage is its size. If we were to get in a wreck, it's old and heavy and sturdy. It'll handle a lot of impact before being damaged."

"I hope you aren't planning any wrecks," he said, leaning over to place Avery in her car seat beside her sister's and buckling them both.

Arden laughed softly. "Nope. And if you'd check out the car, you'd see while it's old, there's not a dent to be found.

That should tell you something about my terrific driving record."

Brendan liked the banter in Arden's tone. He made a production of studying the car, and acting surprised when he found her words to be true. There wasn't a mark on it. He met her eyes over the top when she rounded to the driver's door.

"Looks okay."

She laughed again. He noticed she did that a lot.

"It's in perfect condition, and you know it."

Vague feelings of guilt swept through him as he slid into the passenger side. He studied Arden as she pulled on her seat belt and started the engine. She wore another pair of stretch pants today, the soft white material hugging her long legs. The top she wore was a rich blue, which deepened the color of her eyes. Her hair was pulled back, the only way he'd seen it. When did she release it to flow around her shoulders?

Snapping on his own seat belt, he faced the front, banishing the thought. Flirting with the hired help was not something he even wanted to contemplate, much less start.

Lunch had been a bad idea. They looked like a family. But not the family he'd thought he'd always have. Lannie was gone. Instead, he was standing in line with a tall, leggy blonde with eyes the color of the blue Atlantic on a sunny day. Her laughter was infectious and even people standing near them smiled when they heard it.

She bent over Hailey, listening intently to the little girl's request for lunch. He held Avery again, glad for the warmth of her little body. He couldn't be intrigued by Arden—he refused to be.

The girls ate quickly, more interested in hurrying outside to the play area. As soon as they could, they dashed from the table to the slide and other equipment designed to delight children.

Brendan ate steadily, glancing at his watch. He had plenty of time before he needed to return to the office, but the sooner they were finished, the sooner he could leave and get back to work. He needed something to take his mind away from Arden Glover.

He watched her nibble on a long French fry. He could almost feel her savoring the taste as she dipped it into ketchup again, and took a small bite.

"Are you planning to finish lunch before dinner?" he asked when he realized she ate more slowly than he and his daughters.

She grinned and nodded.

Brendan felt a kick in his gut. She was as pretty as sunshine and the fact that he even noticed concerned him.

"I like enjoying my food, even at a fast-food restaurant. The tastes and textures are to be savored. The flavor relished."

Sensuous, that was the word that popped into mind when he watched her. She seemed to relish everything in life and every aspect, from the visual to the tactile. In the short time she'd been watching his girls, he'd noticed how often she touched them, brushing back a strand of hair, patting them on a shoulder, or hugging them when they said something she liked.

If he said something she liked, would she hug him?

Brendan stood abruptly and gathered the trash.

"I have to get back to the office."

"Already? The girls just began to play."

"I'll walk back to the bank to get my car. It's not far. You stay and take them home when they're finished."

"Yes, sir."

That grin was infectious. Just like her laugh.

Brendan turned and strode away. He needed to gain some perspective. The walk would give him time alone and provide an outlet for the restless energy that seemed to envelop him.

Arden settled Avery in her bed that night and pulled up the covers. What darling little girls Brendan had. Did he know how lucky he was? They were so quiet and polite unless unleashed in the yard. There they ran and yelled and laughed like the children she often saw in the park. Like she had done when she'd played with her friends as a child.

As she had once thought children of her own might one day behave.

"Where's Daddy?" Avery asked again.

Arden smoothed the spread and smiled at the child.

"He's late coming home tonight, remember? He'll be here soon and come up to kiss you goodnight. If you're asleep, he'll still come up."

"Sometimes he goes away on a trip, then he doesn't tell us goodnight," Hailey said from her bed.

"I know. But he always comes home, right?" Arden said, suddenly wondering what would happen if Brendan didn't come home one time.

What would these girls do without at least one of their parents?

The same as she had done, she supposed. Go to live with relatives. They had their aunt Ella, and both sets of grandparents. It wouldn't be the end of the world, just the end of their world as they knew it.

Her own life was full and rich, but she still missed her parents.

Arden wandered back down the steps, the baby monitor in hand. Had Brendan stayed away deliberately? Had it been something she said at lunch?

Or maybe this was just part of his job. His sometimes dangerous, fly-by-the-seat-of-his-pants job. How had he come to make a career of hostage negotiations and top-level security setups? Would he tell her if she asked?

By eleven, Arden gave up waiting. She'd kept a plate warming in the oven but turned off the stove and put the food in the refrigerator. By now, he surely had eaten.

She checked the doors and windows and went to bed.

"Arden?" The knock on the door sounded again.

Disoriented, she rose on one elbow. "Yes?"

"Arden, it's Brendan. Wake up."

She pushed back the sheet and glanced at the clock. It was three in the morning. Crossing swiftly to the door, she opened it. Was there an emergency? Was something wrong with one of the girls?

Brendan stood there, looming in the faint light from the kitchen. He hadn't turned on any lamps in the family room.

"What's wrong? Is it one of the girls?"

"No, they're fine. Still sleeping. I just came home to pack. I'm leaving in a few minutes and need to talk to you before I go. A madman has a family barricaded in a hacienda. We've been working on the situation all night. It's not working. I need to get there in person."

He named a Latin American country noted for instability.

"The local officials have requested my help and I can't say no. I have to leave in," he glanced at his watch, "less than ten minutes. One of the men from the company is waiting out front for me. I'll leave my car here. Use it if anything happens to your old station wagon. Or use the one in the garage. Any last-minute questions? You know where all the paperwork is.

Don't worry about the girls. They already know I take trips."

"I don't have any questions. You left a list of contact phone numbers, I know the routine. I have the papers that give me custody when you're gone. I'll take good care of your daughters. Did you peek in on them? Kiss them goodbye?"

"Yes. They're both sound asleep. You'll be all right with them? If you need anything, call my folks."

"I know, but I won't need them. You'll be home before we know it, right?"

"I sure hope so, but I don't know how long I'll be gone."

Arden didn't know what prompted her, but she flung her arms around him and hugged him tightly. Reaching up, she kissed him lightly on the lips.

"Take care of yourself. Don't be a dead hero. Your daughters need you," she whispered.

Brendan's arms came around her, hugging her tightly, until Arden wondered if he'd ever let her go. A faint whistle from outside broke his hold.

"That's my ride. I have to go."

His mouth covered hers with a fiery kiss that Arden felt to her toes.

Then, suddenly, Brendan was gone.

Stupid, stupid, stupid. Arden groaned as she curled up in her bed a few minutes later and berated herself. How could she have flung herself into his arms? She'd known the man less than a week.

He'd think she was crazy. Certifiable. Or worse, what if he thought she had been coming on to him? Would he have second thoughts about her watching Hailey and Avery?

She closed her eyes, unable to resist reliving his kiss. Her body still tingled in delight. How could the mere touch of lips affect every inch of her? She'd never felt like this before. Maybe it was the lateness of the hour or being wakened from a sound sleep.

Brushing her fingers across her lips, she shivered. Less than a week on the job and she'd jeopardized it. She couldn't afford to lose the position. She needed to make sure she stayed the perfect choice. She had to insure he had no doubts about her capability.

If he brought up the kiss when he returned, she'd pretend she didn't remember. Could she convince him she'd been sleepwalking?

Probably not, he was too astute. Darn, what was she going to do?

Why was she so impetuous? She should have calmly assured him she'd take care of his children while he was gone. And maybe a quiet take-care-of-yourself would have been appropriate.

But no, she had to hug him, kiss him, tell him not to be a dead hero.

Of course, the kiss that had her worried was the one he'd given *her*.

Brendan normally left for work before his daughters awoke, so they were not unduly bothered by their father's absence the next morning. Though Arden expected Brendan spent most of his weekends at home, neither Hailey nor Avery seemed to miss his presence. Even when Arden explained he might be gone for a couple of days, they appeared unconcerned. She was touched that they seemed perfectly comfortable being with her.

Today, she'd take them with her to visit her aunts. Eugenia and Love had called twice since she'd started watching the girls. They were eager to see her and hear all about her new job.

Her phone rang when they were ready to leave. Arden answered, her heart skipping a beat when she recognized Brendan's voice.

"Is everything all right?" he asked.

Noise in the background made it difficult for her to hear him clearly.

"Yes. The girls are fine. Where are you?"

"We just landed a few minutes ago. I'm still at the airport. I don't know how long I'll be tied up. Sometimes these things go quickly, but usually not."

"You are not in danger, are you?"

He hesitated long enough for her to notice before denying it. Was he saying that just to calm her? Was there danger? She had to trust he knew how to handle the situation, but she began to worry.

"The girls are fine. They'll miss you."

"How are you?" he asked.

"Fine." Please don't bring up that kiss.

"I'm sorry about last night. I rarely go around kissing my employees."

His voice sounded husky, self-deprecating.

Exactly the topic she wanted to avoid. Arden took a breath, amazed to find her own voice calm and normal in tone.

"I shouldn't have hugged you. I hope I didn't give an erroneous impression. I mean, I wasn't flirting or coming on to you or anything. It just seemed like, I don't know you were leaving and all."

"I didn't get any impression. You're a toucher, I noticed that with the girls. It was late." He cleared his throat. "Actually, it was sort of nice. To have someone to tell me to take care of myself."

"Oh. Well, good."

She clutched the phone, wishing she could think of something else to say. Did he want to talk to his daughters? She closed her eyes, seeing him as clearly as if he stood before her. Keep safe, she thought fiercely.

"I've got to go. If I can, I'll call later," he said abruptly.

"Don't worry about anything here. I'm responsible, remember? Good luck with the hostages."

"Actually, Arden, you'd be surprised at all I remember."

The connection ended. For a long moment she stared at her phone, trying to figure out just what he meant by that cryptic last remark.

"Are we going?" Hailey asked, running into the kitchen.

"I'm ready," Avery said two seconds later, tagging along after her sister.

Arden smiled at the two girls, seeing their daddy in their features. She refused to get caught up in dreaming about Brendan Ferguson. He'd checked in to see how his daughters were and to apologize for the kiss.

Darn, she didn't want an apology. She thought she might like another kiss.

"Yes, we're ready to leave right now."

She knew so little about Brendan, she mused as she drove to Ocean View. He missed his wife, that she recognized. But it'd been three years. Had he begun to put the past behind him? Had he started dating again or was he still too lost in grief to do that?

Maybe she'd talk to her aunts about him. They were wise and had experienced loss. Maybe they could provide some insight into Brendan's feelings.

And help her avoid any awkward confrontations like that soul-searing kiss. She'd have to watch her impulsiveness from now on. Brendan was not a child to hug impetuously when the mood struck.

As Arden suspected, the aunts adored the children. Hailey

and Avery were quickly chatting away with Eugenia and Love without the normal shyness and hesitation children sometimes showed around strangers.

Eugenia Murray and Love Glover had their own small two-room apartment in the retirement complex, but it was tiny, so they insisted on using the common lawn area for visiting.

"It's warm enough for it," Eugenia commented as she lowered herself awkwardly on one of the white wrought-iron benches beneath a widespread oak. Arden could tell her aunt's arthritis was bothering her. She wished there was something she could do.

Tall and thin, Eugenia's white hair neatly framed her face. Her eyes were the same blue as Arden's and she wore a simple print dress that looked elegant on her.

"We'll get the cold soon enough come fall," Love said as she sat on an adjacent bench. Also thin, Love wasn't quite as put together as her older sister. Her clothes always looked the tiniest bit disheveled. Though always clean, it was amazing how fast they could get wrinkled once she donned them.

"Come sit with me, Hailey, and tell me all about having Arden coming to live with you. She used to live with us, you know," Aunt Love said, patting the space beside her.

"I want you to come visit us often," Eugenia said. "It's not the same living apart as we're doing now. I miss you."

"I'll come as often as I can get away," Arden promised.

"Bring the children. I always loved to be around children. I regret your father didn't have more. A son or two to carry on the name."

"So you've mentioned," Arden couldn't resist murmuring.

It had always been a sore spot. Wasn't she enough? Why had first her father, then her aunts lamented the lack of a son?

"Girls are special," Love said gently, her gaze on Arden. "Your father adored you. You were always special to us from the first day you came to live with us."

Arden smiled at her aunt, the old ache easing a bit.

Try as she might to smooth things out, Love couldn't deny men seem to want a son to carry on their name. Arden had heard it enough growing up.

With two daughters, if Brendan married again, he'd certainly want a son as well. Maybe more than one.

Her friends, Patti and Doug, had discussed when to start their family. Doug wanted a son first, then a daughter.

Sighing softly, Arden shook off her pensive mood. The world was the way it was, and nothing she could do would change things.

The girls ran around the wide lawn, playing tag and shrieking with laughter, stopping from time to time to chat with the different residents, then racing back to Arden to inform her of their brief conversations.

"They're adorable," Love said, watching their antics with a wide smile.

"And they have so much energy," Eugenia added.

"Not all the time. They can be fairly quiet and subdued at home. I was worried I wouldn't fit in that first afternoon. I don't know if that was Ella's influence or not. Their father seems to like a strict routine."

"How does he deal with his daughters?"

"He's crazy about them, but doesn't seem to know quite how to relate. And in the few conversations we've had, it sounds as if his wife took care of Hailey and he had little to do with her. His wife died giving birth to Avery."

"Hmm, most men aren't much use around babies," Eugenia said.

Arden laughed softly.

"That's being sexist. I guess it isn't only men who have definite views along those lines."

When asked to clarify what she meant, she told them about her first night in the Ferguson household, the row with Brendan about his comment about women's work and how she thought she'd almost lost her job before it started.

Eugenia regarded her with some speculation, but Arden knew she'd given nothing away. There was nothing to give away. She enjoyed working for Brendan.

And their kiss would remain her secret.

Chapter Five

The weekend passed swiftly. Arden didn't mind working through her days off. She and the girls had so much to learn about each other, and she loved spending time with them. Their fresh innocence and curiosity were delightful.

In contrast, the early days of the next week seemed to drag. Arden attended her classes, relieved to discover after the first day that the girls really enjoyed the day-care center at the university. They found it to be a treat, which simplified matters.

She had several art projects to complete by the end of the semester and found working on them took most of her free time. So it wasn't a question of being bored.

Yet she thought about Brendan at odd moments during the day. And of course when he phoned each night.

Wednesday, she actually delayed starting her homework after the girls were in bed. Instead, she sat on the sofa, her phone at the ready. He'd called each night at eight-thirty. Since it was his own schedule that had the girls in bed by eight, Arden knew he didn't expect to speak with them.

Which meant he was calling to talk to her.

Her nerves hummed in anticipation. She loved these nightly calls, though she had to admit there was nothing special about them. Each one was predictable. He'd ask after the girls, then she'd ask about the negotiations. When they'd exhausted those topics, there'd be a long silence. She wished she could see him. Guess what he was thinking. Did he want her to talk about something else? Or did he just like having the connection with home?

Then he'd tell her to take care of his children and hang up.

Yet hearing his voice energized her. And gave her that soft feeling in her heart. She'd spent more time talking with him on the phone than they'd spent talking in person. Was she growing to know more about him from the way he described the negotiations? The brief descriptions he gave of the others on the rescue team? Or was her fantasy world kicking in again?

Lost in thought, Arden was surprised when she noticed it was already past nine. Disappointment flared.

He wasn't calling tonight. Not that he had to. It was just that she'd grown used to his calls. He'd probably think she was silly to look forward to them so much.

Slowly, she rose. Maybe things had gotten out of control where he was

Her phone rang.

Arden snatched it up.

"Hello?"

"Arden? It's Brendan."

As if she wouldn't recognize his voice instantly.

"Are you all right?" she asked.

He sounded tired. Was he taking care of himself there?

For heaven's sake, he was a grown man. He'd managed without her his entire life.

"More than all right. We got them all out safely."

"That's wonderful. You did it, didn't you? You talked the man into releasing them. Wow, you must be feeling on top of the world. I'm so glad everything turned out right."

"Yeah, I feel pretty good about it myself."

"I want to hear every detail. What finally caused him to surrender?"

"I can't talk for long. I have to go in just a minute, but I wanted to check in. I'll tell you more when I get home."

"I'm glad you called. When you get home, we'll celebrate. I'll have champagne on ice. And the girls and I will fix your favorite dinner. What do you like best?"

There was silence on the other end for a moment.

"You don't have to do that," he said slowly.

"The girls will love throwing a party. Or don't you normally celebrate major successes like this?"

"I never have."

"Then this can be the first. What's your favorite meal?"

"Steak and baked potatoes."

"Gee, that's original."

He laughed. "We're tied up now in debriefings and in making plans to insure the safety of the family in the future. But I wanted to call you. I knew—"

There was a little static on the line, but not enough to cut him off. Had he stopped talking?

"Knew what?" Arden asked.

"Never mind. I have to go now. I'll be home in the next day or two."

"You don't know when?"

"No. I'll check in and let you know as soon as I do."

"We'll plan the party for Saturday. You'll be back by then, won't you?"

"For sure, by Saturday. Take care of yourself. I've got to go."

Arden replaced the receiver. He hadn't asked about the girls. Of course, it had been a hurried conversation.

Still, despite being caught up in the debriefing and the certain excitement of succeeding, he'd taken time to call her. Smiling, she headed for her room and the assignment that waited.

He'd done it. Because of his skills, a family was free tonight, safe and sound. Her heart pounded as she sat at her table.

Pulling her sketch pad close, she drew furiously broad sweeping strokes to capture Brendan as an intrepid explorer hacking through the thick underbrush of the jungle. It seemed appropriate given where he was, and his cutting through the hostage situation. She could only imagine what he'd look like as a jungle explorer, but she'd always had a great imagination.

It was his face that gave her the most trouble. She couldn't quite capture his expression to her satisfaction. Couldn't seem to put down on paper that air of sadness that appeared at odd instances. But she could draw his virility and energy. And the sex appeal that slowly tantalized her until she wondered if she could ever see him as an employer, as her boss, and nothing more.

Friday, Arden wondered if that would be the day Brendan returned home. His phone call last night hadn't satisfied. She wished he'd finish up quickly and return to Virginia. Being patient wasn't her strong suit. He could return today. He'd said tomorrow for sure.

She had so much she wanted to share with him about his daughters. Hailey and Avery were blossoming. They loved to play outside and had color in their cheeks from their activities.

Both also liked to paint. Once they'd seen her art supplies, they pleaded and cajoled and demanded to be allowed to paint. Arden bought some watercolors, some plain paper, and a roll of butcher paper. Tacking the butcher paper on the long wall beneath the stairs at child height, she allowed them to start a mural. Afternoons, they spent some time outside learning to paint, using the trees and flowers as subjects. Then she'd let them try it on the butcher paper.

Arden put up the fledgling artwork all over the house. It was often difficult to see who was more proud of the work, each artist or Arden.

Hailey had a definite eye for color. Avery liked mixing everything up. But Arden treated each new creation as if it were priceless. She loved to see their proud, beaming smiles when she praised their work.

Friday afternoon both girls were wearing the T-shirts Arden gave them as cover-ups. A thick layer of newspapers protected the floor from drips while Hailey and Avery carefully continued painting their mural. Arden had sketched in trees and flowers and a gingerbread house. The little girls were now adding the color.

Arden sat on the floor nearby, sketching them at work. She loved their concentration. Hailey's tongue peeked from between her lips as she carefully stayed within the lines. Avery mixed colors until she was satisfied with the results, then smeared it on the paper.

The door opened and Brendan stepped in. He stopped, stunned, looking at his daughters painting the wall beneath the stairs.

"What the blazes is going on?" he asked, closing the door ominously behind him.

Arden looked up, her heart catching in her throat.

He was home. And he looked more wonderful than she remembered.

And furious.

Scrambling to her feet, she brushed her hands against her shorts.

"Hi, you're home." Give her extra points for stating the obvious.

He placed his bag on the floor and studied his daughters.

"I can't believe you'd let them paint the wall.

Glancing around, he turned and glared straight at Arden.

"Toys all over the living room, paint on the walls. They're dressed like ragamuffins. Is this how you define responsible, Miss Glover? Girls, put down those paintbrushes and go to your room."

"Wait just a minute here.

Arden motioned to the girls to stay where they were.

Swinging back to Brendan, she placed her hands on her hips and met his gaze without a flinch, her temper flaring.

"If you would take a second and a half to greet your children, and then ask what they're doing, you might have saved yourself from acting like an idiot. I can't believe you'd think I'd let them paint directly on the wall. Do you have such little faith in me? Why ever would you have hired me if that's what you think I'm capable of? We're painting a mural on butcher paper, not directly on the wall."

"Butcher paper?"

She nodded and glanced at the girls. Both were watching their father with wide eyes.

"Go kiss your daddy hello, sweeties. I bet he's glad to see you," Arden said in a gentle voice.

Her narrowed-eye look at Brendan warned him he better act like he was glad to see them.

"I am glad to see them. I don't need someone to tell them that."

"You could have fooled me," she murmured as the girls ran to greet their father.

He kissed them, ruffled their hair, and then asked them what they were wearing.

"It's our painting smocks," Hailey said proudly. "We wear them to keep our clothes clean."

"Mine's blue," Avery said, leaning against Brendan's leg and watching him with adoring eyes.

"It looks like it swallows you up," Brendan said, raising his gaze to Arden. "I'm tired. I've been making snap decisions for days. There was no need for me to overreact when I walked in the house, however. My apologies."

She nodded, feeling somewhat placated. He looked tired.

And the strain of the last few days must have been tremendous. Lives had depended upon him.

"The toys will be picked up before dinner. We'll have the paint put away by then, as well. If we'd known you were coming home this afternoon, we wouldn't have started painting."

Looking closely, she could see the lines of fatigue around his eyes, bracketing his mouth. The rest of her anger vanished instantly.

Avery raised her arms, and Brendan leaned over to pick her up. He nuzzled her cheek, and she laughed. For an instant, Arden felt almost jealous.

Impossible. Why wouldn't she want him to show affection to his daughter?

She wished he'd show some to her.

"Want to come upstairs with me and help me unpack?" he asked.

Hailey nodded, racing back down the hall to put her brush in the jar of water.

In only seconds, Arden was left alone in the hallway. She listened to the murmur of his voice, the childish laughter. Feeling left out, she cleaned up the paints. The girls would be occupied with their father for the rest of the afternoon. They'd paint again another day.

And she wasn't disappointed. She wasn't.

He had no reason to single her out to give her a special greeting. The phone calls had just been his way of checking in each day. They had meant nothing special to him.

But for one lonely moment, Arden wished he'd kissed her hello and told her he'd missed her.

Brendan put the last of his clothes in the hamper. Hailey hadn't stopped talking for a single second. He listened with half an ear, still berating himself for that display downstairs. He shouldn't have lashed out like that.

But the sense of joy that had hit him when he entered the house and saw Arden and his children had been unexpected. And unwelcome. She was merely his daughters' nanny. Not someone he had any interest in. Not someone to feel glad to see again.

Avery bounced on his bed, trying to interrupt Hailey and tell him her version of the event. Both girls were talking and laughing and making reference to things he didn't recognize. Arden would know.

But he could try to figure it out. Bemused by the change in his quiet daughters, he tried to follow their rendition of how they spent their days. It was unexpected, seeing such an appreciable change. But he liked it. He didn't understand it, but their personalities seemed to sparkle.

A direct result of Arden's influence?

Thinking about her brought her image to mind again. He could see her rising from the floor, all long legs and graceful movement. He clenched his hands into fists and tried to concentrate on his daughters.

But the memory of Arden's long legs filled his mind. And her hair. He was becoming obsessed with wanting to see it when it wasn't tied back. She even slept with it that way, if the other night was anything to go by.

He should have been ready for the impact of seeing her again. Hadn't he called every night while he was gone just to talk with her, to hear her laughter, the sound of her voice?

"I did that one. Do you like it?" Hailey said, pointing.

Brendan looked at the wall. Two drawings were posted side by side.

"That's mine, Daddy. It's pretty, isn't it?" Avery said, jumping on the bed, her hand going up and down as she pointed as she jumped.

"No jumping on the bed," Brendan said, sweeping her up and holding her over his head.

She shrieked with laughter. He held her close, wanting to protect her from the ugliness of the world. He sat on the edge of the bed and pulled Hailey close.

"Tell me again about the pictures," he said.

He had to pay attention. Time enough later to sort through his thoughts about Arden. This was time for his children.

When Brendan descended the stairs sometime later, the hallway had been cleared except for the fledgling mural. He stopped to look at the sketches, then smiled at the coloring that had been started. Did their amateur childish work bother the artist in Arden?

He continued into the kitchen, stopping in the doorway to watch her. She didn't know initially that he was there. Her back was to him and he enjoyed the view while he could.

Long tanned legs moved back and forth as if she danced to a secret melody, her hips swaying seductively. Her hands chopped vegetables, moving quickly. He hoped she didn't cut herself. Her blond hair was pulled back, the ponytail swaying with her movements.

The memory of their kiss swept through him, making him forget everything else but the thought of doing it again.

Which was probably the best way he knew of scaring her away. He needed her for his children, not for himself.

"I take it you're the one I have to thank for the new artwork on my bedroom wall?" he said.

She spun around, knife flashing in the light.

"Oh, you startled me."

She studied him warily for a minute, then relaxed.

"Yes. Do you like the pictures? I thought the walls needed some more color, and what better source?"

"I never considered myself a connoisseur of modern art, but I guess I can learn."

She laughed, and he felt a sense of well-being sweep through him. He liked her laughter.

"Not so modern as merely childish. Avery especially likes to mix all the colors until she gets a muddy greenish-black."

"I noticed. And they seem to be everywhere."

Arden nodded. "But we rotate them. They paint at the rate of about one per minute sometimes, so we needed to establish a plan. Otherwise, the walls would be plastered from floor to ceiling with paintings."

He liked the *we* in her statement. It showed she was relating to the girls. That was good.

"If my unexpected arrival throws off your schedule, I can eat out."

"Don't be silly. I'm making stir-fry. I'll just cut up more veggies and we'll stretch the chicken. You must be tired. I bet you can't wait to go to bed."

Her words startled him. For the first time since Lannie died, Brendan thought about taking someone else to bed–Arden Glover.

The image shocked him. He wasn't interested in getting close to anyone again. Losing his wife had caused too much pain to ever risk such heartache again.

He had his business, his children. His life was complete.

But he wasn't sure his body realized that. It suddenly seemed to have a life of its own and insisted he pay attention to the demands it made.

He wanted Arden.

"I suppose you want to talk about it," she said, turning back to the vegetables.

Talk about wanting her? Talk about taking her to bed? Were his thoughts so obvious?

"The way I've altered the schedule you had for the girls," she said when he didn't speak.

Brendan leaned against the doorjamb and crossed his arms over his chest. Mentally, he breathed a sigh of relief. For a moment, he thought she could read minds.

"How much have you altered?"

"Quite a bit, I'm afraid. I, uh, am not much into regimentation."

"Neither am I, but children like routine. Lannie said."

"I'd never contradict what your wife said. However, Hailey was younger than Avery is now when she died. As children grow and change, they need new boundaries and new routines. And to be allowed to explore and discover the world. What worked for a two-year-old won't work for a child almost ready to start kindergarten."

It made sense. But Brendan scarcely gave it the attention it deserved. He was startled to discover talking about Lannie didn't cause the searing pain it once did.

Chapter Six

Today was Saturday and Arden intended to have her aunts visit. Aunt Love had promised to show the girls how to make thumb print cookies. She wondered if she needed to alter the plans since Brendan Ferguson was home. Sipping her morning coffee, she gazed over the backyard, trying to decide whether to ask his permission or just carry on.

Brendan came down to breakfast dressed in a suit. The girls were still sleeping.

"Are you going out?" she asked hopefully.

If he was gone for the day, she'd have free rein around the house. Not that she thought he'd object. She wouldn't have invited them if she thought he'd mind. The girls loved her aunts and if they made cookies, they'd have something special for dessert.

"I know this is your day off, normally. But if you could watch the girls today, I'll take a day off later in the week and spend it with them. I really need to go into the office today."

"That's fine. I didn't know you'd be back, so I made no plans except for dinner tonight."

And for the baking party. They'd have some cookies for dessert.

"Dinner?" he asked.

"Celebrating the success of your mission."

He looked at her for a moment.

"I wasn't sure you meant it."

"Of course I did. I wouldn't have suggested it if I hadn't meant it."

"I appreciate your watching them today. Did you need me for anything here before I leave?"

The coolness in his tone struck her at odds with the man she'd talked with every night on the phone. For a moment she wished she could recapture the warmth of each call.

"Not at all. You will be here for dinner, right?"

He nodded.

"Where are the girls? Shouldn't they be up by now?"

He checked his watch.

"They'll be along when they wake up. I don't think children should be on a strict schedule."

"You mentioned that last night. They are, however, *my* children. And I decide how to raise them. Routine is important."

"That's the point. They are *children*. Give them love and attention and they'll be fine. I don't mind watching them today, but you'd want to spend some time together with them. They haven't seen you in a week."

"I'll spend time with them this evening. One way I take care of them is to make sure I can afford this house, live-in help, nice clothes."

"Things," Arden said, waving her hand dismissively. "They want attention from you."

He gazed at her for a long moment, his eyes narrowed.

"I have to go."

Arden stared after him. Was the thought of spending time at home so awful he couldn't even take time for breakfast? She frowned.

He seemed to genuinely love the girls. And last night he'd demonstrated a marked amount of patience with their endless questions and chatter. But there was something almost like he was unsure how to talk to them, except to answer questions.

And he'd seemed startled when Avery had crawled into his lap after eating and asked him to tell her a story.

"Hi, Arden. I'm hungry," Hailey said, walking slowly into the kitchen.

Arden looked up and smiled. The day would begin in earnest now. If Hailey was up, Avery would follow any minute.

Brendan threw down his pen and stared out of the window. He found it difficult to concentrate. There were plenty of reports to read, decisions to make, correspondence to answer. His secretary had left everything just the way he liked it. And he enjoyed his work.

But today he kept visualizing the young woman who was

watching his children.

He wasn't sure what he'd been expecting when he returned home last night, but it hadn't been the strong urge to sweep her up into his arms and kiss her, to wrap himself around her and absorb her lightness, her laughter, her sunny outlook.

After days of delicate negotiation with people's lives in the balance, he welcomed the serenity and safety of his home. That was all.

Scowling, he rose and paced to the window. The view was one he was used to, other office buildings, a couple of small trees by the sidewalks. The sky was a clear blue. The day promised to be hot.

What was he doing here instead of being at home with his children? Arden was right he should spend time with them.

But that might entail spending time with their nanny, and he was reluctant to do that.

He didn't like the feelings that were stirring within him. He'd loved his wife. Yet the feelings he felt around Arden were different. He was attracted to her. What red-blooded man wouldn't be? Yet, she was as opposite to Lannie as a woman could be. If he'd been asked, he would say he liked petite, dark-haired women.

Yet just thinking about Arden had him envisioning scenes that should be x-rated. He'd been on the edge all week, and now that the danger was past, he was feeling the anti-climax.

That's what was causing his wild imaginings.

He headed for the door, grabbing his suit jacket as he passed the coat rack. He'd finish up on Monday. Today, he'd spend the afternoon with his children and ignore the allure of his nanny. By Monday morning, he'd be back to normal.

"Let me," Avery said, pushing Hailey.

"It's my turn." Hailey stood her ground, sheltering the mixing bowl in her arm.

"Avery, it is Hailey's turn. You had a turn. Now you must wait," Arden said firmly, scooping up the little girl and resting her on her hip.

"There will be plenty of turns," Aunt Love said as she patted Avery's cheek. "Don't go through life being so impatient."

Arden laughed. Like a three-year-old can be any other way. She looked up and froze. Brendan Ferguson stood in the doorway to the kitchen.

"I thought you were working all day," she blurted out.

She cringed at the mess everywhere. Flour dusted the girls' clothing and faces. A light dusting coated the counters and the floor. Dozens of cups and bowls were haphazardly stacked around. Each child had her own mixing bowl for the brownies that were now baking. The delicious aroma filled the room.

Aunt Eugenia looked up from rolling out the cookie dough. She glanced first at Brendan, then swiftly at Arden.

"Is there a problem?" she asked.

"Come on in, young man. Though watch out for the flour, wearing that dark suit. Maybe you should change first. Then you can join us," Aunt Love said genially.

"Hi, Daddy," Hailey said, beaming at her father. "We're baking cookies. It's my turn to stir."

"I want a turn," Avery said from Arden's arms.

"I see," Brendan said.

It was clear from his expression this was not the scene he'd expected to come home to.

"Arden, may I see you for a moment?"

Without waiting for a reply, he turned and walked down the hall.

Arden sighed.

"Guess I better go explain. Here, Aunt Love, can you take Avery?"

Arden dusted as much flour from her as she could and then headed out to the front of the house, looking for Brendan.

"He stood in the living room, near the front window, staring out over the pristine front yard. Hearing her, he turned to look at her, his expression unreadable.

Arden plunged into speech.

"I hope you don't mind me inviting my aunts to visit. They miss baking, not having a kitchen anymore. And the girls love it. They took to it like a duck to water. We'll have the kitchen spotless by dinnertime. Anyway, I thought you'd be at work all day."

"While the cat's away?" he asked.

"No, of course not. We've had this planned for a few days. You are welcome to join us, but I think Aunt Love is right. You need to change first. We're not exactly the neatest cooking crew in the world."

Brendan's gaze ran over her, and Arden felt that quickening sense of awareness. She wished she wasn't covered in flour. Wished she had put on makeup and an outfit that would show off her figure to advantage.

Not that it seemed to matter.

"Brendan?"

She met his gaze, hoping the confusion she felt didn't show.

"Come and bake cookies with your daughters. They'd find that a treat. And you can meet my aunts."

He hesitated, then nodded.

"I'll be there in a few minutes."

The glimmer of a smile showed.

"If I'm going to end up looking like you, I need to change into my oldest clothes. Do you try to wash them when you're done, or would all the flour clog the washing machine?"

She laughed.

"We'll brush everything off and run around outside before we change. That'll take care of the worst of it. You'll love watching Hailey and Avery during their cooking attempts. They insist on tasting the batter at every turn, each wants to do more than they know how yet, and neither one can measure ingredients worth a darn. But they love it. And it's good for my aunts, too."

He stepped close enough to reach out and raise her chin with the edge of his hand.

"And you, doesn't it make extra work for you?"

"A little. But it's worth it. Days like this will make special memories. Childhood should be full of special memories, don't you think?"

He was silent for a moment, dropping his hand and turning toward the stairs.

"You don't want to know what I'm thinking right now, Arden."

She watched until he was out of sight, hoping the pounding in her chest would slow down. Hoping the color wasn't as high in her face as she suspected it might be. She didn't want to give rise to speculation by her aunts.

Brushing her jaw with unsteady fingertips, she shivered. The heat spiraling through her from his touch was exciting. And scary.

She had her life mapped out, and it didn't include getting sidetracked into a dead-end relationship. She knew her limits, and daydreaming about her employer was dangerous. Exciting, but perilous to her peace of mind and her future.

Ruefully thinking she was too late to chastise herself, she returned to the kitchen. Keyed up, she could hardly wait until Brendan joined them.

"Everything all right?" Eugenia asked, looking at her shrewdly.

"Sure. Brendan's changing, then will join us. Won't that be fun, girls? Daddy will help."

"Goody." Hailey said, dipping a finger into the batter and dripping on the counter as she tried to transfer it to her mouth.

Arden smiled at her aunts and tried to hide her nervousness. What if Brendan wanted the place cleaned up as they worked rather than when they were through? Or criticized the children making such a mess? They were not proficient, but the happiness shining from their eyes was the real reason for baking.

She hoped he wouldn't put a damper on things. She wanted the day to be special for Hailey and Avery as well as for her aunts.

Her worries proved unfounded. When Brendan joined them a few minutes later, he seemed to fit right in, or as much as a six-foot, four-inch male could who knew no more about baking than his daughters did. Charming in his greeting to her aunts, he asked them questions that soon had them chatting away with ease.

He admired Hailey's stirring and watched in silence as Avery helped Aunt Love take the brownies from the hot oven.

"She won't let Avery get burned," Arden murmured, coming to stand near him. She didn't want him to worry.

He glanced at her, his eyes dancing in amusement.

"Are you here to reassure me? I think I can tell what care your aunt takes. She's great with the girls. They both are. Your aunt Eugenia is the one with arthritis, isn't she?"

"Yes, but she tries not to let it slow her down."

"When do we get to eat the brownies?"

"After they cool down. Are you going to try your hand at cutting out some cookies?"

He nodded. "Going to show me how?"

"Can't you remember back that far?" Arden teased.

He shrugged. "My mother rarely baked. We usually had store-bought desserts. I don't ever remember baking cookies at home."

"Then follow me, sir, and I'll show you all I know."

"Now that sounds tantalizing," he said, low enough for her ears alone.

Arden felt that flutter in her heart, the dancing of sensation cross her skin as he stepped closer and leaned against her shoulder as she pressed the cookie cutter into the dough already rolled flat.

"You're crowding me," she said.

"Hmm?"

She turned and almost bumped into him. His face was mere inches from hers. She could clearly see the faint lines radiating from his eyes. The gray in his gaze was warmer than she'd ever seen. His breath brushed across her cheeks. A few scant millimeters closer and her lips would touch his.

Time seemed to stand still. She felt the blood racing through her veins, felt the now-familiar warmth invading every cell. The room faded and for a long instant there were only the two of them, in a world of their own.

The memory of their goodbye kiss a week ago rose, bringing all the sensuous awareness it had evoked.

What would happen if she lifted her head slightly and let her mouth meet his? His lips would be warm and firm. Would he sweep her into his arms, molding her body to his, and ignite the flame of passion?

She almost gave in to the craving of her body to touch this man, to taste him, feel his strength and give in to the desire that grew by leaps and bounds.

Gazing into his eyes, she was mesmerized by their change to silver as the answering flare of desire rose.

"Arden."

It took her a second to recognize her aunt's authoritative voice.

Blinking, she turned to look at Eugenia. "Yes?"

Her aunt gestured toward Avery.

"The child is waiting for you to put the cookies on the cookie sheet."

Embarrassed heat washed through her as she realized

everyone in the kitchen was staring at her and Brendan.

Good heavens, had she lost her mind?

"Oh, Avery, I'm sorry. Here, let's bring your stool closer and you can stand up here by me. I've already cut out a couple of cookies. I'll get the rest in just a second. You can help, too."

"Okay."

The little girl's delighted smile warmed Arden's heart.

She did her best to ignore Brendan. To ignore what almost happened and in a room full of relatives. She knew she'd hear more about this from her aunts. She hoped the girls hadn't picked up on anything.

At a normal debriefing session after a crisis situation, Brendan mused, he and the others analyzed the entire operation to see what they'd done right and what could have been handled differently. In this case, he had a list of what he could have done differently. Should have done differently regarding his girls' nanny.

Trying to concentrate on cutting the cookies and placing them on the sheet his daughter was guarding, he reflected on the different steps that led him to where he had almost forgotten that his daughters and Arden's aunts were present and swept Arden into a passionate embrace. Which, unless he was way off base, she would have joined in wholeheartedly.

The phone calls had been a mistake. That started it. If he hadn't talked with her each night, would he be so interested?

So relaxed in her company?

Relaxed? Hardly. She had him tied up in knots.

He looked at her. She was doing her best to avoid his eyes. Scanning the room quickly, he noted her aunts did not seem unduly perturbed by the scene. They continued to talk with Hailey and Avery. And with him.

Not Arden. She was silent, which definitely was an unusual behavior for her. He missed her constant chatter.

Maybe it hadn't started with the phone calls. Maybe it had started with that kiss. Which one? The chaste one she'd given him or the fiery one he'd been unable to resist giving her before leaving?

"Or it could have started at the interview," he murmured.

"What?"

Arden looked at him.

He shook his head. "Nothing, just thinking aloud."

"Oh."

Quickly her gaze skirted away.

Great, now she wouldn't even look at him. *Nothing* had happened. Why was she acting this way?

And the reason nothing had happened, he asked himself. Not because he'd done anything to prevent it. He'd almost leaned forward and brushed her lips with his. His hands had itched to cup her cheeks. Feel the softness of her skin. He'd yearned to brush the flour from her chin and become lost in the blue of her eyes.

He shifted, glad the island counter was high enough to hide his body's reaction. Being near Arden was causing all kinds of problems.

Focus, that's what was needed. He was here to spend time with his daughters, not lust after their nanny.

"Okay, who wants a turn cutting out the cookies?" he asked.

Chapter Seven

L ooking at the mess in the kitchen, he knew his father would have a fit if he ever saw it. But he wasn't his father and his daughters seemed to be having the time of their lives. They'd never remember their mother, but he could give them happy memories of their childhood.

Arden was wise beyond her years, he thought as he began to relax and enjoy the afternoon with Avery and Hailey. Making happy memories *was* important.

Eugenia began washing the bowls.

"I can do that, Aunt Eugenia," Arden protested, coming to stand beside her at the sink.

"I like the warmth of the water on my hands, child. Remember, Love is the cook, I always cleaned up. But you can help. Find a drying cloth."

Arden was grateful for the task that took her away from the center island and gave her some space. Drying the bowls, she stacked them on the clean counter beside the sink. Who would have suspected they could use so many for just a few batches of cookies?

Eugenia added still another bowl to the soapy water, glancing around the kitchen for more. She smiled.

"Brendan is as dusty as his daughters," she murmured.

She glanced at Arden. "He's a fine young man."

Arden nodded. She knew to her aunt's eighty-some years, Brendan must seem young. But he was eight years older than she was and he had a wealth of experiences she didn't.

"He seems to relate well with his daughters," Eugenia continued.

"When I first arrived, they seemed very formal," Arden said slowly.

"Of course, such a virile man needs some sons, too. I can't see him playing football with those dainty little girls. Or taking them to ball games."

Arden took a deep breath, trying to stave off the hurt. She knew her aunt would be shocked to learn how her words hurt. She was just sharing an observation. But to Arden, it again reminded her of why there could be nothing between Brendan and her.

If he ever married again, he'd want a woman who could give him healthy sons. Boys to play with, to roughhouse with, to teach manly things. And boys to perpetuate the family name.

"Does he come from a large family?" Eugenia asked.

"He has a sister. He's never mentioned any other siblings."

"That's right, Ella, isn't it? The one who used to watch the girls before you?"

Arden nodded. That was what she had been hired for to watch the girls. The job gave her the opportunity to pursue her education at the same time she worked. She refused to jeopardize it by falling for her boss.

It was late afternoon by the time the last batch of cookies finished baking. The girls had long since gone down for a much-needed nap. With the kitchen back in order, and the delicious aroma of cookies filling the house, Arden felt more in control.

She sought Brendan, finding him in the den, working on his computer.

"Can you keep an ear out for the girls? I think they'll sleep a little longer, but if they wake up, make sure they don't get into mischief."

"Where are you going?" He looked up from the computer.

"To take my aunts back. I'll be home in time to cook dinner."

"Aren't they staying for the celebration? The more the merrier, isn't that how it goes?"

"I hadn't planned on them staying. I don't have enough steak."

"Then zip out and get some more. I'll entertain them until you return."

Quickly saving his work, he rose.

"Are you sure?"

It was one thing to have her relatives over to bake cookies with the children, something else again to all sit down to dinner together.

"I'm sure. If your family has had these celebration events before, we'll need their input to make sure this one goes perfectly."

Arden laughed softly. "Brendan, it's just a dinner with a few extras to make it special. I think the girls and I could manage that much on our own."

"Ah, but there's nothing like experience. Go buy some more food, Arden."

"Yes, sir," she said with a mock salute.

Dinner proved to be festive and entertaining. Arden dressed the girls up in their best outfits and then donned one of her own she usually saved for Sundays. The aunts grumbled about their clothes, but their summer dresses looked fine, once the flour had been sponged off.

Brendan dutifully followed suit, donning a sports coat, but foregoing the tie. If he was the celebrant, he told Arden, he got some perks.

The girls had each drawn a picture of their daddy, the hero. Arden had also sketched a drawing of Brendan a phone in one hand and a sword in the other. His eyes gleamed when he looked at her after receiving the picture. She knew he, too, remembered their phone conversations.

Eugenia and Love contributed stories of previous

celebration dinners, recounting events in their lives and Arden's that kept everyone enthralled.

After telling about Arden's honors in high school, Eugenia turned to her. "Isn't that right, Arden?"

But Arden had missed the story. She was picturing another sketch, one with Brendan and his daughters. This time she could envision him surrounded by clouds of flour and dirty bowls piled higher than his head. The enchantment in Hailey's and Avery's eyes would balance the scene. She ought to use dark clothes to emphasize the contrasting white of the flour.

"She gets like that," Eugenia said indulgently.

"Spaces out?" Brendan asked, studying Arden.

She was looking at Hailey, but he didn't think she was seeing her.

"Whenever she's thinking of a painting," Love explained. "I've missed that."

Eugenia nodded. "Happens at the oddest times. She'll get a notion and want to paint it, so goes into almost a trance as she decides how she will do it. Right, Arden?" She ended in a louder tone.

"What?" Arden looked at her aunt.

"I was telling Brendan that you go into a trance if you are planning a picture."

"Oh." She glanced at him almost guiltily. "Sometimes."

"And does he know you often stay up all night working

on a painting?" Love asked teasingly.

Arden shook her head.

"I won't while here. I know I have to be up early to deal with the girls. You don't have to worry about me neglecting my duty," she told Brendan.

"Were you thinking of a painting just now?"

She nodded. "One of Hailey and Avery." And you, but that part she'd keep to herself. Her fingers itched to get to her sketch pad.

It was late by the time the aunts had been driven home, the girls put to bed and Arden escaped to her room. She thought she heard Brendan call her, but ignored it if indeed he had. She needed time and distance.

And the soothing familiarity of her sketching. Her charcoal pencil flew across the page. Sketch after sketch poured from her. Brendan on the phone in some phantom city in Latin America. Brendan cutting cookies with Avery. Brendan laughing at something Aunt Love had said. Brendan seriously attending the steaks on the grill.

Tired, Arden lay back, flexing her fingers. Glancing at the clock, she was shocked to see it was after three.

Scrambling to gather all the sketches, she put them in a large portfolio and tied it tight. The work was good, but she would have done better to have gone straight to sleep. It'd be morning before long.

Still keyed up, she tried to relax. Turning off the light, she stared into the darkness. Even in the black of night, she could see Brendan's face, remember their kiss, feel the craving for another.

Turning on her side, she tried to ignore the clamoring of her heart as she drifted off to sleep.

Arden awoke Sunday morning aware it was the first day since she'd moved to the Ferguson place she was not responsible for the girls. Delighting in the knowledge, and the unexpected sense of freedom, she planned all she'd do on her day off.

First, she'd treat herself to breakfast at the restaurant near her aunts' retirement home that offered dining on the terrace overlooking the water. She'd buy the Sunday paper and take her time reading, eating and enjoying quiet time alone.

Then she'd pick up her aunts and drive them to church in their former neighborhood. They'd all like to see old friends. Maybe they could stop for lunch at the cafeteria near the university. She'd call Patti after taking her aunts back to their home to see if she wanted to go to a movie.

With the entire day ahead of her, Arden took her time getting dressed. Before she was ready, she heard her charges thundering down the stairs. Smiling, she wondered again how two such dainty little girls could sometimes make such a racket.

In deference to the warm weather, she wore a cheerful

primrose yellow sun dress. White sandals showed off the pale pink polish on her toes. She pulled back her hair to allow her neck to stay cool. She'd stop by the kitchen on her way out, to let Brendan know she was leaving and to tell the girls goodbye.

When she walked in, Avery and Hailey were seated at the kitchen table eating cereal. Brendan stood by the counter, pouring himself a cup of coffee. Her breath caught for a moment when she first saw him. He wore shorts and a sleeveless T-shirt. The muscles of his obviously fit body were clearly displayed again. Sleek and masculine, he embodied all she'd ever imagined in the perfect male physique.

Once more, her fingers itched to sketch him in some pagan pose, displaying all the masculine beauty of his form. But a slow curl of heat deep within also had her imagining more than just sketching him.

She'd like to run her fingertips over every inch of him. Touch him, caress him, taste him. Explore the difference between his body and hers. Venture into a new realm of physical sensation as she discovered what it'd be like to give in to the awareness that built every moment they were together.

Taking a deep breath, she smiled, hoping it looked somewhat friendly and non-revealing.

He heard her intake and looked up. His eyes darkened slightly as he narrowed them, letting his gaze move from her face down her body. Arden felt as if he'd touched her, heat spiraling through her in the direct path of his gaze.

"I'm off now," she said as the seconds ticked by.

He nodded.

"Where are you going?" Hailey asked.

"It's Arden's day off. She's going out and where is not our business," Brendan said, turning to his daughter. "You and Avery finish eating breakfast."

"I want to go."

"You can't. Arden gets some time to herself."

"You'll be all right?" Arden asked, suddenly hesitant to leave.

He nodded, his gaze meeting hers.

"I can be back in time to make dinner," she offered.

"No need. We're going to some friends' place today. They are having a barbecue. We may not be home until after dark. I appreciate your willingness to help us out on your day off. Very commendable."

She shrugged. It wasn't just a sense of responsibility. She wondered how he'd manage cooking for the three of them. Now she didn't have to worry. He was their father, granted, but he seemed at a loss sometimes with how to handle the girls. But his plans showed he didn't need her today at all.

"Unless I get an unexpected call in the middle of the night again, you're on your own until tomorrow morning," he said, leaning against the counter, crossing his arms across his chest.

Arden nodded, not taking her eyes off him. He looked solid and substantial, leaning there with quiet male assurance.

She had to get going, or she might ask to stay to spend her day off with him. And his daughters, of course.

Brendan watched her kiss the girls goodbye and leave. He remained leaning against the counter as if he didn't have a care in the world, appalled at the sensations that were churning through him. He wanted to kiss her again. Sweep her into his arms and lock his lips with hers until the world went away, leaving them in a cocoon of their own.

She looked beautiful, tall and slim and sexy as anything he'd ever seen. The dress floated and swayed as she walked, faithfully outlining her delectable figure and those long legs.

He listened to her car start, then fade as she drove away. Where was she going? With whom would she spend the day? He wanted to know. Not that he could come up with any legitimate reason to satisfy his curiosity. It was none of his business, just as he'd told Hailey. Maybe he should have let his daughter persist.

Not that knowing that would dampen the desire to touch her, be with her. Listen to her conversation, delight in the way she viewed the world.

He rubbed the back of his neck, pushing away from the counter. There were a dozen things to see to and two little girls to watch. He had no time to be fantasizing about Arden Glover.

Easier said than done.

Brendan suspected it'd prove to be a long day.

It was after ten that night when Brendan and the girls returned home. His friends had young children as well, and the kids ran around and had a great time.

Paul wanted to know all the details about the recent mission, and Brendan waited until they could be alone after dinner to discuss what he could.

Since it had been late when they left, both girls had immediately fallen asleep in the car.

Turning into the driveway, he was pleased to note the lights on in the house. And to see the old station wagon in its place in the driveway. Arden was home.

When he stopped the car, she came out of the side door.

"You said after dark, but I was starting to wonder if you were coming back tonight," she said.

She'd changed to shorts and wore a skimpy top. He couldn't tell the color in the evening darkness, but he could see enough of her outlined by lights behind her to know it was formfitting. Swallowing hard, he climbed from the car.

"We left later than I planned. Both girls are asleep. I'll carry them up, but no bath tonight."

"I'll take Avery, and you can carry Hailey," she said, going to the back door of the sedan.

Brendan nodded. It was a sensible plan. But for a moment he remembered another time, another house, another woman. They'd returned home from visiting their friends when Hailey had been a baby. She'd been asleep and Lannie had reached in to carry her up to bed.

Arden looked nothing like Lannie, yet the scene was one of family. Parents carrying their children into their home. Closing the door to the world and keeping their family safe in their own haven.

He scowled as he climbed the stairs. Where in the world were such fanciful thoughts coming from? He wasn't some poet. And he certainly wasn't planning on another wife.

Arden was hired to watch his children, and that was all. When they were older, other arrangements could be made.

And three was a family. He'd make sure it was the best family the girls could ever have.

"Thanks," he said gruffly when she tucked up Avery after removing her sandals and dusting off her feet.

"Did they have fun?" she asked, touching Avery lightly, as if reluctant to leave her.

"April had a wading pool for the kids. They have two around the same age. They played in it all afternoon."

"I bet they loved that. We've played in the hose a couple of afternoons. I thought I'd take them to the beach sometime. Hailey says she can swim."

"Ella taught her last year. Avery was too little."

"I expect she'll catch up soon. She loves to do what her older sister does."

"There's time enough."

Brendan looked at his daughters. They were so small, so precious.

"And did you have fun today?" Arden asked.

He looked up and into her pretty blue eyes. For a moment Brendan forgot about his visit, forgot he was in his daughters' room. All he could think of was how pretty Arden looked and how much he wanted her.

Slamming the brakes on those longings, he looked away and nodded once.

"It's late. I don't want to keep you up. Thanks for carrying Avery," he said.

"No problem. Goodnight," she said, slipping quickly from the room.

Had that been disappointment in her tone? Hurt?

"I don't need this attraction," he muttered as he followed, switching off the light.

Tomorrow, things would get back on an even keel. He'd be in the familiar routine of work. The girls and Arden would be back in their normal habits and this aberration would fade.

At least, he hoped so.

Chapter Eight

What did you expect? Arden asked herself as she went to the kitchen to prepare a glass of iced tea before going to her room. They weren't friends. He didn't have to tell her anything about his day or ask about hers.

He'd made that perfectly clear. She didn't have to be told twice about something. From now on it was strictly by the book. Exactly like her friend Patti said he liked it.

Burning with indignation and embarrassment, she went to her room and closed the door, full of determination to make sure there'd never be a hint of the longing she felt. If he wanted just a nanny for his children, so be it.

She wouldn't offer a friendly ear in case he wanted to talk. She wouldn't take an interest in what he was doing. And she definitely wouldn't miss spending time with him.

Liar, her mind whispered.

She sipped her tea and plopped on the chair near the window. There was little to see in the dark summer night. The trees shaded the yard, blocking most of the starlight. The lights spilling from the house illuminated only a few feet before the dark shadows claimed the night.

Maybe he'd go on another trip and phone each night. She smiled ruefully. Was that the only way she'd get to talk to him? For a moment, she considered calling him up just to ask about his day. Would it make a difference?

Did she want it to make a difference? She had her life mapped out with no time for side trips. And this job was perfect. She'd best do nothing to jeopardize it.

On Monday, Arden put her plan into action. She went to her classes, took the girls grocery shopping and made sure the house was spotless and dinner was on the table promptly at six that evening.

She refrained from speaking directly to Brendan unless he asked her a specific question, and made sure she never made eye contact. It helped contain the fluttery feelings inside, but even without once looking directly at him during dinner, she was fully aware of his presence.

On Tuesday, she and the girls took a picnic lunch to a park while the cleaning crew took care of the house. She delayed painting on the mural until Wednesday, when they'd have time to clean up before Brendan arrived home. Dinner was perfect when again they ate on his time schedule. Once or twice during the meal she felt Brendan's gaze on her, as if puzzled. But she devoted her attention to the children and did her best to ignore him and the sensations that seemed to escalate every time she was around him.

By Thursday afternoon Arden was going slowly crazy. Sitting in the backyard while the girls played tag, she leaned against one of the trees and closed her eyes. The stress of following the strict schedule was driving her nuts. And did it matter? Brendan probably hadn't even noticed. Or cared.

Every night this week he'd been home in time for dinner, and then spent the evening in his den working. He was missing valuable time with his daughters.

Not that they seemed to find anything amiss. Was that their normal pattern? See their daddy at meals and the rest of the time stay out of his way?

She felt isolated and cut off. What had happened? He'd kissed her. They'd almost kissed last Saturday when baking. She'd asked a couple of questions, but nothing earth-shattering.

It wasn't too much to expect some quiet adult conversation in the evenings, was it? At least at mealtime. Surely he talked with Ella.

Arden's heart began pounding. Maybe her technique was faulty. Maybe she should encourage conversation between father and daughters and gradually introducing conversation between themselves.

She wanted to know more about Brendan, how he thought, what he felt. How he had made hostage rescue and high-level security a life's work. What plans and dreams he had for his daughters.

And she couldn't deny that shimmering awareness. At first, it had come when he entered the room. Now, she had only to think about him and it manifested itself. Was it only one-sided?

People kissed for different reasons. What were Brendan's reasons for kissing her?

Did he want to kiss her again?

"I'm tired, Arden," Avery said, coming to sit down beside her and leaning against her.

"I guess so, sweetie. It's way past nap time. Want to take it out here in the shade today?"

Avery looked around. "Outside?"

Arden laughed and hugged the darling child. "Why not? I'll bring out a nice blanket and spread it out here in the shade. You can sleep right here beneath this nice tree. I'll lie down with you."

"And Hailey?"

"Yes, and Hailey."

"What?" Hailey asked, running over to drop to her knees beside her sister.

"We're going to take a nap here in the shade, won't that be fun?" Arden told her.

"In a tent?" Hailey looked around.

"No, darling, not in a tent. Right here in the open. We'll spread a big blanket and each get a pillow. We can look up at the leaves before we fall asleep."

Hailey looked around again. "I never slept outside before," she said slowly.

"Then we'll have a new adventure," Arden said with a laugh.

Sometimes these girls were too quiet and lacking in an adventurous spirit. Children should be spontaneous and full of excitement, clamoring for new escapades.

A few minutes later they were settled in the shade of the large old oak. Arden told them stories as they gazed up through the leaves at the clear blue sky while dappled sunlight brushed their cheeks.

Before long, all three were sound asleep.

Arden awoke first. She hadn't meant to sleep away the afternoon, but after working on her end-of-the-year art projects after the girls were in bed, and then lying awake long afterward each night thinking about Brendan Ferguson, it was no wonder relaxing in the peaceful afternoon air produced such a result.

Refreshed, she still lingered, enjoying the soft melody of birds in the late afternoon, the caress of the air as it moved gently along in a sweet breeze, the closeness she had with these adorable little girls.

The sound of a car door in the driveway had her sitting up suddenly.

She checked her watch. It was later than she thought.

Brendan was home, and she hadn't even thought about supper, much less started something. Scrambling to her feet, she hurried to the house, trying to come up with an idea of what to prepare that would be quick. She couldn't let him find her sleeping away the afternoon.

She dashed into the kitchen just as Brendan entered from the dining room. She stopped short and looked at him, sure her guilt was clearly obvious.

"Is there a fire?" Brendan asked lazily, taking in her flustered look.

She shook her head, took a deep breath, and smiled brightly.

"I was just checking on the children. They're napping in the yard."

He glanced around the kitchen. "No dinner started?"

Arden looked around, stalling. So much for following his routine.

"Um, I thought we could have a picnic tonight. Grill burgers on the barbecue. Make ice cream," she improvised.

"Make ice cream?"

She nodded.

"You have an ice cream maker, don't you?"

He shook his head. "Not that I know of."

"Oh. I thought everyone did."

He stared at her, and she wondered if something was wrong. Did she have grass in her hair? Or a leaf tangled in it?

She knew she probably looked a mess. It wasn't fair. Even after a full day at the office, he looked cool and immaculately turned out.

"Is this a spur-of-the-moment plan?" he asked.

She nodded. "Spontaneous. Children need spontaneity in their lives. Grown-ups, too, for that matter."

He stepped closer. "All grown-ups?"

She nodded. "I believe so, don't you? It gives an extra fillip to life. Think how boring things would be if we did nothing but the same old thing day after day."

"Routine things, you mean?"

He stepped closer.

Arden felt that familiar flutter inside. Her mind was starting to short-circuit. How close did he plan to come?

"Yes. No. I don't mean routine is boring, necessarily."

Wasn't he the one proposing a schedule for his children? She couldn't insult him.

"But if there is routine, then it's even more important to have some spontaneity."

"Spontaneity." He nodded.

He was close enough to touch. Close enough to feel the heat from his body invade her space. Arden swallowed hard and stepped back to find the counter at her back. He took another step closer.

"I wondered how long routine would last," he said, reaching up to brush a tendril of hair off her cheek, tuck it behind her ear.

Arden's knees threatened to give way.

"You did?" she squeaked, her gaze caught firmly in his. His eyes seemed to change from cool gray to a smokey silver that captivated.

"All last week on the phone you told me of the wild and definitely non-routine things you and my daughters did," he said. "This week, everything seems different. Predictable, routine."

"I thought you wanted that," she said breathlessly.

Her skin felt too tight. The delicious tingling from the spot his hand touched swept through her.

"I like order, but not necessarily life without some imagination."

"Oh."

Had he taken all the air? Was that why she was having such trouble breathing?

"I like the idea of a picnic dinner. That's innovative and sounds like something the girls will love."

She nodded, her gaze dropping to his mouth, watching him talk. She wished he'd kiss her again. What could she do to let him know that without being totally out of line?

Probably nothing, but she'd think of something. She had to, or go slowly mad.

Not only the thought of a kiss would drive her insane, however, it was the way the man blew hot and cold.

"You're confusing me," she murmured.

He became still. "How so?"

Shrugging, she sidestepped around him until she was free. "I don't know what you expect, Brendan."

Frowning, he slid his hand into the pocket of his trousers and looked at her.

"What do you mean?"

"Expect from me."

"I want you to watch my children."

"And is that all? Before you left, you kissed me like—"

She stopped. She didn't need to tell the man it had been unlike any kiss she'd ever received.

"Well, it was really super. And then Saturday when my aunts were here and all—" she stopped again.

"A couple of kisses. Are you telling me you've never been kissed before?"

"No. It's more than kisses. You called and talked every night you were gone. And not just about the children, though we started that way. Then Sunday I felt as if you'd ordered me to stay away don't ask questions, don't expect anything."

"Arden, I don't—"

She raised her hand. "That's fine. I mean, whatever you want, just make it clear. But now, right now, I'm not sure what's going on."

"Right now, I want to kiss you. Do you want me to?"

She swallowed, afraid she'd imagined his comment.

"But it can't mean anything," she protested.

He reached for her and pulled her closer, resting his hands on either side of her neck, using his thumbs to gently tilt her head until she was only inches from his. Slowly, his thumbs caressed the line of her jaw.

"It can mean two people like each other and like what being together can do for them. I enjoy touching you, kissing you. It won't go any further. I'm not looking for an affair or to get involved again. And didn't you tell me you weren't interested in a permanent relationship? Was that true or just words?"

Her hands grasped his wrists, but she didn't know if she wanted to pull his arms away or hold on for dear life.

Nodding slightly, she said, "I'm not looking to get involved in a relationship. That part's true. I'm never getting married. And I can't have an affair with you."

"I never asked you to."

"Then I guess I wouldn't mind another kiss," she said in a rush.

There was something wrong with the logic here somewhere, but she couldn't figure it out right now. Brendan Ferguson wanted to kiss her, and Arden felt her day would not be complete if he didn't.

She closed her eyes when his lips touched hers.

"Is Arden hurted?" Avery asked just as the screen door slammed behind her.

Arden and Brendan jumped apart.

"What?"

"Oh, honey, no I'm not hurt."

"Why was Daddy kissing you to make it better?"

Swallowing hard, Arden looked at Brendan.

"You field that one. I'm going to get started on making hamburgers."

Embarrassed heat flooded through her. What if he had kissed her, really kissed her instead of a brushing of lips?

What would they have done if Avery or Hailey had seen them?

Affection between relatives was important. But she and Brendan weren't related. And never would be. She didn't want to give the wrong impression to anyone.

But the disappointment that swelled was hard to contain. They'd been so close. So wondrously close. If only Avery could have slept just a few more minutes. *If only.*

Arden wondered what impression they'd present to an outsider if someone watched dinner that night. It was an immense success. The girls faithfully stood by their father watching him grill the meat with total concentration and fascination.

Not that Arden blamed them. She'd like to sit and watch Brendan, too. But she made a quick salad, gathered the condiments, set the card table and carried out the drinks.

Keeping busy made more sense, and kept her from silly daydreams.

After they ate, they all piled into Brendan's car to go to the ice-cream parlor. No ice-cream maker had been located to try homemade. Arden wondered if she could find one somewhere and have it the next time she got the notion. She knew the girls couldn't turn the handle once the ice cream got solid, but they'd love to take a turn at the beginning. And they could always add the salt and ice as it melted.

For a little while, Arden let herself imagine it'd always be like this. Brendan talking to her and the girls, the children excited and laughing, her own heart full and content.

If she stared at his mouth more than she should have, she hoped he didn't notice. If only Avery had slept just a bit longer, she'd have got to plunge into a deep kiss that probably would have rocked her world.

Chapter Nine

It was after nine by the time they returned home. Arden wondered if Brendan would comment on how late the girls were up. It was definitely a break in routine. But it was summer, and another happy memory had been made. Arden considered it well worthwhile.

She bathed them and had them in bed when Brendan came up to tuck them in.

She kissed the girls and started to leave, startled when Brendan's hand grasped her wrist.

"Don't go yet. I'll just be a minute."

She watched as he bid each child goodnight and tucked them in with a kiss.

They left the room together, reminding Arden of parents, of family, of things she'd probably never experience once she left the Ferguson home.

"We have some unfinished business," he said as they walked down the stairs.

Unfinished business? The kiss.

"Do you want to sit outside?" he asked unexpectedly.

"That sounds good. It's a lovely night."

It'd be even better if she could keep two coherent thoughts in her mind. But his closeness seemed to draw the focus of every cell in her body. His shoulder bumped hers lightly as they walked. He shortened his stride to match hers.

They sat at the makeshift table, glasses of iced tea still sitting in condensation.

"I meant to discuss this with you earlier, but we got sidetracked," he said, leaning back in the flimsy chair and stretching out his legs. He was quiet for a moment, then he looked at her.

"I have to go to Washington on business next week. I'll be gone a couple of days. At least we have some advance notice this time, and I'll leave at a reasonable hour."

She smiled and nodded. "We'll be fine."

Arden fidgeted with her glass, taking a sip of the last little bit of tea, feeling the cold ice press against her lip. Too bad she couldn't let it cool her entire body.

"Then there's something else," he said.

She set the glass down and stared at him, puzzled by the odd tone of his voice.

"What?"

"I have a dinner party to attend at the end of next week. Would you go with me as my plus one? I know it's not part of your job description, but I'd rather take you than someone else."

She held her breath. Brendan wanted to take her to a party? Introduce her to friends and colleagues?

"As a *date?* Brendan, you practically ignored me this week. Now you want me to be your plus one at some party. I thought we were getting to know each other a little better on the phone last week, then everything changed over the weekend. You blow hot and then cold. How does that relate to me going to a party with you?"

Surely she was misunderstanding.

"It's more of a business arrangement. We discussed the situation earlier. Neither of us is looking for more than friendship. And since we both know the score, no false expectations would be raised. It seems if I invite a woman to accompany me to a business event, she immediately thinks there's something more. I usually take a plus one so not to be odd man out. Often it was my sister, but I can't do that anymore."

She let her breath out in a whoosh. Glad for the darkness that hid her expression, she hoped her voice sounded normal.

"Probably a wise plan. No misunderstandings, and you'll have an even number at the table."

She would *not* feel disappointed. Hadn't they both said earlier that neither one of them wanted anything to develop? Men and women usually went as couples to parties. If he needed to attend for business, she'd be glad he invited her instead of someone from his office.

"I'm happy to help. How formal is it?"

"Dressy. If that's a problem, I can buy you a gown."

"It's not a problem. I have dresses."

She frowned for a moment, looking at him, wishing she could see him clearly even though she was glad for the shadows.

"Still, won't your bringing me give rise to gossip?"

"I don't know why it should. Most of the people know I have a nanny for the girls. We're living in the same house. We can't help but spend some time together, get to know each other. And to help each other out if the occasion warrants."

"But not have an affair," she said firmly.

She needed to be very clear on that point because she was totally confused about everything else.

"Right."

He was silent for a long moment. Then he raised his eyes until he gazed directly at her.

"You know I don't want to get involved. I've been clear about that from the get go. So no false hopes raised. I won't go through losing someone I care about again."

He shook his head impatiently.

"Not that I don't care about you, Arden. I do. You're pretty and funny and vivacious and bring a breath of fresh air to this house. To this family. I like that."

"But not enough to pursue a relationship," she said shrewdly.

"It's not that so much, as an attempt to banish the unsettling feelings I get when you're around. That's why I've tried to keep my distance from you this week," he said softly.

That was unexpected. Was this attraction two-sided?

Slowly, she began to smile. Her eyes danced with amusement.

"And did it work?" she couldn't resist asking.

If so, she'd take a page out of his book and try avoidance techniques.

He shook his head.

"So the next best thing is try to be friends?" she asked wryly.

"Do you have a better idea?" he asked.

"No. Are you hoping familiarity will breed contempt? I'm willing to try if you are."

Impulsively, she leaned forward and kissed his cheek, then stood.

"Now that we've settled that, I need to get to work. I have an art project to finish by next Tuesday. It counts for a huge percentage of my grade."

He stood as well. "You're going in? I thought you'd want to talk some more."

"I need to get to work on my project. These evening hours are essential for me. I can't work on the projects while the girls are up. Don't you usually bring work home with you?"

He nodded, reaching out and pulling her closer.

"Thanks for helping me out on Saturday," he said.

With that, he swept her into his arms and kissed her.

Arden closed her eyes in startled surprise. Two seconds later, she relaxed and gave herself up to sheer pleasure. She wound her arms around his neck and kissed him back with all the pent-up passion that she had in her.

The world seemed to tilt, to spin, to shower them with a kaleidoscope of rainbow colors.

Both of them were breathing hard when they slowly pulled apart. Arden let her hands trail across his shoulders, down along the strength of his chest. Fingertips tingling, she finally broke contact.

The dark hid his expression, could he see hers?

"Goodnight," she said breathlessly. Turning, she almost ran to her room.

Or was she floating? It was hard to tell.

She closed her door and drifted to the window. Was he still outside? No, the yard was empty.

Turning, she caught sight of herself in the mirror, eyes bright blue, cheeks flushed, lips rosy and damp.

And heart racing a million miles an hour. Slowly, she smiled.

It was several long minutes later before she calmed down enough to work on her project.

On Friday, Arden and the girls continued painting the

mural in the afternoon. Hailey and Avery loved to paint and would have gone on well into the evening, but Arden wanted to clean up the mess before Brendan arrived home.

She'd have made it if the house phone hadn't rung. It was Ella. She and her husband had arrived in California and she missed the girls and wanted to talk to them.

Hailey and Avery had so much to tell their aunt, they were more than an hour on the phone. They were still talking when Brendan walked into the kitchen.

Arden looked up, shot through with guilt, conscious of the mess left in the hallway. How late was it?

"Are you home early?" she asked, glancing at the clock. It was an hour earlier than his normal arrival time. "Are you sick?"

He shook his head, an eyebrow raised in question as he glanced at the girls.

"It's Ella. She's in California."

"Ah."

He kissed Hailey, lifted Avery while she was talking, and smiled at her.

"Can I have a turn to talk to Ella?" he asked.

Avery finished her story and then almost hit Brendan in the head with the receiver as she swung it away from her ear.

"It's Auntie Ella," she said. She squirmed around until Brendan put her down.

"Hi, Ella, how did the move go?"

Arden headed for the hall, purposefully leaving the Ferguson family alone. She had a few minutes to get the painting mess cleared up. Working swiftly, she was pleased at the way the children's imagination was captured with their painting. While she stayed to be with the girls when they talked on the phone, she didn't need to be part of the family once Brendan was home.

For a moment she felt a pang of regret. Sadness that she'd never enjoy a close family relationship. That she could never have a child or grandchildren. That her home wouldn't ring with laughter or the thundering of feet dashing down stairs.

Maybe she'd take the mural with her when she left, to remind her of the happy days spent with Hailey and Avery.

Enough, she admonished. She'd known that was the way it'd be since she had been a teenager. She was comfortable with her plans for her future. What couldn't be changed had to be dealt with.

In the meantime, she was crazy about Brendan Ferguson's girls. They were bright, funny, and delightful to be around. And she thought she was bringing something to them that had been missing–a sense of adventure and gaiety. Not to mention art appreciation.

"I wondered where you went to," Brendan said, walking into the hall.

He studied the mural.

"Progress, I see. It's more than half completed. And I can spot Avery's efforts a mile away."

"I planned to get everything cleaned up before you came home, but you're early, and they were having too much fun to quit."

Hands full, Arden glanced his way.

"Afraid of my reaction to the mess?"

His eyes danced in amusement.

"Something like that. I know you like order and neatness and I didn't want to get on your bad side," she said with a grin.

He laughed.

"Right. I don't think so. Something tells me you're afraid of very little."

"Hold that thought. Why are you home so early? I haven't even started dinner."

Brendan slipped his hands into his pockets and rocked back on his heels.

"I'm the boss, so I decided I could take time off if I wanted."

He had no intention of telling her the real reason that he'd been impatient to see her again.

"Want to go out for pizza tonight?" he asked.

It was a treat Hailey especially loved. He knew that his explanation for asking her to his business event last night seemed flimsy. He was glad she hadn't pushed for a stronger reason.

Like an explanation for that strong physical attraction, a voice whispered. He clamped down on the thought.

"I'll change and we can head out," he said.

"Don't feel you need to include me. If you want to take the girls out, do it. I can get something for myself."

She headed for the kitchen, one hand balancing the water cups, the other holding the damp rag and two brushes, with the folded newspapers held beneath one elbow.

"I want all of us to go. I wouldn't have invited you if I'd only wanted it to be the girls and me."

For a moment, he wondered if she'd refuse. The terms of the job were such that if he were home, she was no longer on duty.

Perhaps she'd rather not eat with them.

"Then I'll get the girls ready. Thanks."

She smiled almost shyly and disappeared into the kitchen.

Brendan remained standing in the hall, his gaze moving back to the mural. He refused to analyze the feeling her smile engendered. Focusing on the positive aspects, he was glad to have her here with his daughters. He like the way she was expanding things, like the painting they seemed to love.

He was intrigued by her. She seemed carefree and flighty sometimes, yet showed great patience with his children. And her devotion was obvious, even after so short a time. She hadn't come with the background he wanted, but she suited.

More than he'd expected.

Frowning at that thought, he headed for his room.

He and Arden could enjoy a business relationship that let them share things like a night out for pizza with his daughters. He'd do the same with any woman who was watching his children.

And the kisses?

Chapter Ten

The pizza parlor was crowded. Teenagers chatted in groups and couples laughed and called to each other. Young parents chased after children or sent the older ones with quarters to the video room. Here and there, an older couple ate quietly, watching all the activity in bemused fascination.

The aroma was savory. The noise was loud. The commotion was total confusion.

From the smiles on everyone's face, it was perfect.

They ordered a large cheese pizza and soft drinks, and Brendan found a table near the rear. As soon as they were settled, Hailey wanted to go play the video games.

"Can she really play them?" Arden asked in surprise.

"Not exactly, but she loves the race car one. I'll take her. Sorry, I forgot to mention her delight in the games."

"Avery and I will guard the table. But if the pizza arrives before your return, it's everyone for herself."

Brendan nodded, brushing his hand lightly against her shoulder as he and Hailey headed for the video room. He wanted to do more, but kept a tight leash on his impulses. He knew better than anyone it could go only so far.

Once they were used to being around each other and the novelty wore off, he hoped the proclivity to want to spend every waking moment with her would wane. Not to mention the non-waking ones.

It was hard to talk over the noise, but when Brendan and Hailey returned, Arden asked how it had gone.

Hailey regaled them with her driving, and Brendan added an aside or two to clarify the situation.

When the pizza arrived, the girls cheerfully began to eat and watch the other customers in the huge restaurant.

"Tell me how you got into the security business," Arden asked as she nibbled her first piece.

Brendan scooted his chair closer and took a large slice. He shrugged.

"I started in the hostage negotiation end of things after law enforcement training. If a person can avoid getting snatched, there is no hostage situation. So I began looking at how high-risk people could beef up security."

"Were you a cop? Dealing with hostages?"

"FBI. I left the agency when I married Lannie. She didn't want an agent for a husband. We both liked Norfolk, so settled here. At that point, I could have started my company anywhere, so this is now headquarters."

"Wouldn't somewhere else have more high-risk security clients? I mean, I don't exactly think of Norfolk, Virginia, as the most dangerous place to live. I'd think more of New York or L.A."

"You're right. It's one of the safer cities in America. A good place to raise a family. I go where the work is, but prefer to live here."

"So when you go to Washington next week, it's for work?"

"Checking in with some clients. Keeping in touch with friends."

"With friends still in the FBI?"

He nodded.

"Some of them refer my services. I don't want to dry up that angle. But most of my business comes by word of mouth."

"And the family in Latin America, the one you freed. Will they be hiring you for security?"

"They already did before I left. I have a team down there now."

"How many employees do you employ?"

He looked at her, eyes narrowed. "At work? Seventy full-time and another fifty on an as-needed basis. One at home."

"Is that enough?"

"It's enough for me to keep tabs on what's going on, and yet be able to meet the demand of our clients. We continue to grow, but I want to make haste slowly. Every step is rock solid before we expand."

"Planned and scheduled," she murmured, remembering

the way he wanted his household run.

"Not much room for spontaneity there," he agreed. "But," he reached out and used his thumb to brush a dab of tomato sauce from her lip, "there may be room for spontaneity in other aspects of my life."

Her heart skipped a beat. She pulled back, trying to put enough distance between them to forget the heat of his fingertips, the feel of his thumb as it touched her. She needed something to gain some perspective.

Despite her best efforts, she wondered if she was getting in over her head. Almost three weeks working for the man and she could hardly remember her life before. And she was certainly having trouble holding on to her plans for the future.

A future that would not include a sexy hostage negotiator and his two adorable children.

If she felt this way after three weeks, what would she feel like in three years when her time was up?

Probably head over heels in love with the man.

The thought came out of the blue and shocked her.

"Excuse me, I need to, um, use the ladies."

Arden shoved her chair back and stood, wanting to run from the restaurant. To run for her life.

But she knew she couldn't do that. Still, she needed a minute to herself.

She walked swiftly through the dining crowd and found the restrooms. Grateful for a few minutes alone, she stood near the sink, searching her features for a clue about what to do.

She couldn't be falling in love with Brendan. There was no future in that.

"He's still in love with Lannie," she said slowly.

Arden couldn't afford to fall in love. Not with anyone who wanted more than she could give.

"Maybe he doesn't," she said hopefully to her reflection.

Two teenage girls came giggling into the room. Arden turned on the water and began washing her hands. She couldn't stay hidden in here all night.

"I'll go out and act normally. Once we get home, I'll have some serious thinking to do. Can I stay? Or had I best get out now, while the going is good?" she murmured beneath her breath.

She rather thought it was too late. Leaving wouldn't erase his image from her mind. Leaving wouldn't change the feelings which exploded inside her whenever she thought about him. And leaving certainly wouldn't enable her to follow through on her plans to graduate before she was twenty-eight.

As she walked slowly back to the table, dodging rambunctious children, she thought about the dozens of sketches she'd drawn of Brendan since she'd met him. Maybe just living in the proximity of any virile man would have her concocting fantasies, no matter who he was.

Yet one look at him sitting at the table laughing with his

two little girls, and she wanted to hurry. She didn't want to miss a second of time she could spend with him. And her hands itched to sketch the family as they talked and laughed, the remains of the pizza scattered on the table.

He looked up as she joined them, his eyes concerned.

"Is everything all right?"

She nodded with a bright smile. She'd make it through this and one day look back on it with nostalgia. There was nothing to say. She couldn't keep in touch with the girls once she left. See them every so often.

Keep track of what their father was doing.

She sat down and reached for her soda.

"Did you have enough to eat?" Brendan asked.

"Yes, it was delicious. I see there isn't enough to take home. I suspected as much. You seemed to like it a lot."

He nodded, his eyes still assessing. "We haven't been out for pizza in a long time. Sometimes Ella would order in."

She looked at the girls, afraid to look at Brendan now that she was so aware of her feelings for him.

"Do you have plans for the weekend?" he asked after a moment.

"I might go to the beach tomorrow," she said slowly.

"I want to go. You said you'd take us. Can we go, too?" Hailey said, picking up instantly on the word beach.

"Tomorrow is Arden's day off. She doesn't take care of you on her day off," Brendan said.

"Why don't you all come? We could take a picnic lunch and rent an umbrella and make a day of it. I'm sure the girls would love to play in the water and make sand castles," Arden suggested.

And she'd love to see Brendan in a bathing suit, actually see the body she'd been fantasizing about for weeks.

And spend time with him.

He didn't refuse immediately, but she could see it coming. Why not just throw herself at him, she thought in disgust.

"Can we, Daddy? Can we?"

Hailey almost bounced in her chair, she was so excited. "We haven't been to the beach in a long time."

"I want to go," Avery said, picking up on her sister's enthusiasm.

"Not tomorrow," Brendan said at last.

He looked away.

"I have things to do to prepare for my trip next week. I was planning to work at home this weekend."

"I can still take them, if you like," Arden offered.

Disappointment seemed to be a constant with her lately. She smiled at Hailey and Avery.

"I'll take them tomorrow and you'll be able to work as much as you want without being interrupted."

"I can't ask you to do that on your day off."

"You didn't, I'm volunteering. I think it will be fun. If you get finished early, I'll let you know where we'll be and you can join us."

Saturday seemed to drag by. Brendan put in the time on the projections he needed completed for the upcoming trip. Then he wandered around the house, feeling its emptiness.

He'd known last night he dare not join Arden and the girls at the beach. He needed to keep his distance to keep his sanity. And seeing Arden in a bathing suit was a sure-fired way to forget all about distance. But the day seemed empty and long with all of them gone.

As he studied the drawings that Arden had scattered in every room, he was struck by how different the house looked—far different from the immaculate showplace Lannie had kept. Would she have hung up Hailey's work? Displayed it proudly so their daughter felt cherished? He thought so, if she let Hailey draw something.

He picked up a doll and placed it on the sofa, sitting beside it. Closing his eyes, he leaned back. It was hard to remember what Lannie looked like now. Every time he tried to envision her, Arden's face danced behind his eyes. Her laughter echoed in his ears.

She was vibrant and had a zest for living that was infectious. He wondered what her paintings were like. And was she truly resigned to go the commercial art route or did she secretly long to paint for the sheer joy of it?

He rose and wandered into the family room. Arden had left her door open. It wasn't prying if he didn't go in the room.

He stood in the doorway and studied the changes she'd made.

Two pairs of shorts were on her bed as if she'd been trying to decide what to wear that morning. A large canvas stood facing the window on an easel, where it'd get the most light. He was curious to see what she was working on, but there was a limit to his comfort level in invading her space. On the dresser was a sketchbook, flipped opened. He couldn't quite make out the figure she'd drawn. It looked like a Viking. Was that for her project?

He leaned against the doorjamb, conscious of the fragrance wafting through the air. It was Arden's. He studied the bottles on the dresser, wondering which was her perfume and what it was called.

Suddenly, he wondered if he'd been a fool to pass up the chance to spend the day with her. To see her laughing with his daughters, racing them on the sand, and building fantasy castles near the water's edge.

But what he missed most was the chance to see her in a bathing suit, water glistening on her skin, her hair wet and clinging to her neck. The glow of perfect health radiating from her as she smiled at him.

Next time, if there was a next time, he'd go. He could

handle the attraction that seemed to flare between them. She'd done nothing untoward in the presence of his children. A day at the beach would be fun.

It was late afternoon when they returned. Brendan came from his home office just as the girls raced into the house. Their cheeks were rosy, sand trailed behind them.

"Run upstairs and we'll take a bath first thing," Arden was saying as she maneuvered inside carrying a beach ball, two soggy towels, and a beach bag.

Her cheeks were rosy as well. The top and shorts she wore covered her, but the damp spots visible let Brendan know she had pulled them over her wet suit.

"Hi, Daddy," Hailey veered toward Brendan. "We had the bestest time at the beach. We made a gigantic castle and Avery chased crabs. And then Arden said we brought half the beach home with us, but we didn't. It was a very big beach."

"I almost catched a crab, but it went in the hole," Avery said, running to overtake Hailey.

Brendan could see the fine glitter of sand on her arms and legs. He could imagine what Arden's old station wagon must look like.

Raising his gaze, he looked at her. "Sounds like a perfect day."

She grinned and nodded. "You should have come. We could have used your help on the castle. Upstairs, girls. Time for a bath before dinner."

They headed up the stairs, stomping like they were a small herd of elephants. He stared up as they disappeared from view.

Brendan turned and looked at Arden.

"I don't know how to relate to little girls that much. I think maybe I would have done much better with sons."

Sons. What was it with men? She'd heard that all her life, first from her father, then her aunts, from Patti and Pete and now Brendan.

Turning quickly, Arden climbed the stairs. She loved these two little girls. And she knew Brendan did as well. Yet he felt he could relate better to boys. If he'd spend more time with his daughters, he'd relate fine.

They were making strides at dinner. He asked questions that had both Avery and Hailey opening up and sharing their day with him. And he seemed to enjoy it.

Her heart dropped. Her aunt had been correct. If he ever married again, he'd want sons to carry on his name.

Sons to relate to.

"Arden?" Brendan called.

"I have to give the girls a bath."

"Come back down when you're finished."

She waved in acknowledgment, but had no intention of spending a moment longer with the man than she had to.

Despite her best efforts, she had fantasized about a relationship between them. She was falling in love and there was no future in it. Even if he ever got over losing Lannie, she couldn't marry him, knowing she could never give him the sons he wanted.

She needed to keep her distance and get over this *infatuation* as quickly as she could.

Final exams were coming up next week. She would devote her energy to studying, completing her project, and focusing on her course work. Maybe she could take a few classes this summer to hasten her graduation.

Arden prepared a quick, cold supper of sandwiches and fruit salad. The girls told their father all about their day at the beach, laughing and interrupting each other in their excitement.

Brendan listened without interruption, watching them with a hint of bafflement in his eyes. Twice he looked to Arden for clarification.

Which he probably wouldn't have needed to do if they were boys, she thought grumpily as she reluctantly shared the explanation of the activities they'd done at the beach.

"I should have gone," he said at the end of the meal. "It sounds as if you all had a great time. Although I got a lot accomplished for my trip."

"Yes, you should have come with us. I think the girls would have found it much more enjoyable. And you can't work all the time."

He nodded. "Next time you go, I'll go, too."

"Or you can take them yourself next weekend."

Arden looked away. She wouldn't be joining in any more family activities. His comment today made it clear to her that she had better focus her attention on where she had a future not in futile endeavors with Brendan Ferguson.

Chapter Eleven

Before dinner was over, Hailey asked if Brendan would watch a movie with them before bed that night.

"What movie?"

"Frozen?" she asked hopefully.

"I'd love to watch the movie with you two."

He glanced at Arden. "Will you join us?"

She shook her head. "I'm tired, I think I'll go to bed early."

She didn't meet his eyes, but continued to concentrate on clearing the table and then doing the dishes.

Of course, the television was in the family room with just the thickness of a door from her. She could hear the excited voices of the children, Brendan's quiet tones. Then the murmur of the movie.

When the smell of popcorn wafted in, her mouth watered. She'd eaten plenty of dinner, but there was something about the aroma of popcorn that had her wanting some.

Trying to ignore the enticing image on the other side of the door, she went to the drafting table to study her project. It was a design implementation as a prototype for one of her classes. Almost finished, it didn't take long for Arden to be caught up in her project as she put on the final touches.

Pleased with the work, she carefully rolled it up and put it in a tube to protect it. Now what? The movie still droned on. Were the three of them cuddled together on the sofa? Or had Brendan sat in the chair and left the sofa for the girls?

She longed to peek out, but instead drew her sketch pad closer and began drawing a picture of Brendan and his daughters on the sofa. His hard features were softened as he looked at Hailey. Avery snuggled against his side while she placed Hailey a little apart, telling him of their day.

Arden studied the drawing when she finished. She'd captured the excitement in the children's expressions and the bafflement Brendan sometimes displayed around his girls. Flipping over the page, Arden began to sketch another.

It was late when she put her pad down and stretched.

She was still wide awake, but a glance at the clock showed it was after midnight. Listening for a moment, she heard nothing. Everyone else had gone to bed hours before.

She rubbed her eyes. They felt strained after hours of sketching. And the results of her work were for her eyes only. She wouldn't share pages of pictures of Brendan Ferguson with anyone.

Standing, she rotated her shoulders to loosen up. Maybe one day, in the distant future, she'd have a showing at an art gallery and could frame some drawings. She loved the one where she'd depicted him as a Viking warrior. And the one in the flower garden with two dainty little girls. That one she'd like to paint, maybe using oils. Watercolor would be too weak.

"Yeah, right, your own showing. They don't show commercial art," she scoffed.

Pacing her room, she decided to take a walk in the yard. Maybe the cool night air would clear her head. Then she'd try to go to sleep. She should be exhausted, but she felt full of energy.

Punching in the security code on the panel by the back door, she let herself out into the yard. Looking directly overhead, she could see the vast array of the stars in the night sky. The trees blocked a panoramic view, but she could see enough to fill her with delight. There was no moon, just the black canopy sprinkled with a million points of light.

It was a balmy night, with just a hint of a breeze. She wandered around the yard until she grew cool. Time to go inside and to bed.

Stumbling over one of the girls' toys, she almost fell. She nudged it aside and headed for the house. Pausing for a moment on the stoop, she looked up again at the stars. Maybe one night she could take the girls to the beach after dark and let them see the entire sky as black as velvet with the scattering of a billion stars.

She turned to go inside, pulling the door behind her.

Suddenly she was grabbed from behind.

"All right, what are you doing here?"

Brendan's harsh voice sounded in her right ear.

"Brendan, it's me, Arden. I live here," she squeaked.

He turned her, his hands hard against her upper arms. She reached out and touched bare skin. Snatching her hand back as if she'd been burned, she tried to see him in the darkness.

"Arden? What are you doing outside at this time of night?"

"I couldn't sleep. I thought I'd just get some fresh air. Is that a crime?"

"No. Of course not. I heard something, came downstairs and found the door open. I know I closed it and set the security alarm before I went up. When I saw you come in, I thought, well, never mind."

"That I was a burglar?"

She almost laughed.

"At least we know we'll be safe when you're home. You must be a light sleeper."

"I wasn't asleep."

"Oh.

She was conscious he still held her, but his hold had changed from capturing to almost caressing?

She could feel the warmth from his body envelop hers. Daringly, she reached out and touched his bare chest again, her fingertips exploring the expanse of skin. At last she had direct contact with those muscles she'd longed to trace and explore. His skin was hot, the muscles rock-hard beneath.

Opening her palm, she pressed it against him, stepping closer, breathing in the very essence of Brendan. Her heart skipped a beat and then settled down in a rapid tattoo.

"I didn't mean to worry you," she said softly, entranced by the shivering sensations that filled her, the tingling in her hands that seemed to zip through her entire body.

"Why are you still up?" he asked.

She shrugged. "I worked on my project, finished and then drew whatever picture I wanted for a while. When I realized how late it was, I stopped, but still needed to unwind. So I stepped outside for a breath of fresh air. Now I need to get to bed."

And step away from temptation. But her feet refused to move.

"You work too hard. You should have gone to bed early like you indicated you were," he said.

This from the man who worked all day on a Saturday?

"So what's your excuse for still being awake?" she asked.

"Habit."

"Habit?"

He took a deep breath. When he let it out, it ruffled her hair.

"When Lannie first died, I used work as a means to forget. To keep my mind occupied, so I didn't have to think about her. Now it's just a habit. Fill the hours with work to keep from thinking, missing."

"You need to spend more time with your daughters. Wait," she said before he could respond. "You said earlier you couldn't relate to them and would feel more at ease with a boy. That has nothing to do with their being girls, you know. You need to spend time with them. Find out what they like to do. Teach them things they want to learn. They can play ball or learn to swim, or whatever you think is appropriate."

"They're so little. I'm afraid of any rough-and-tumble in case they get hurt."

"They won't break if you use some sense. Run with them, laugh and play. But most importantly, spend time with them. These are precious years that, once gone, won't ever be back. You need to build memories to last a lifetime. Give them memories to last their lifetimes."

His hand moved up her arms to her shoulders, then to cradle her head, his fingers rubbing in her hair, releasing the clasp that held it back, spilling the cascade of curls into his palms. His fingers caressed each strand as if it were silk.

She was having trouble breathing again. Did he have a clue what his touch did to her?

"You'll have to show me how, Arden."

"How?"

She was confused, captivated, entranced. What was he talking about?

"Show me how to be a good father," he said, brushing his lips across hers. "Spend time with us to make sure I'm getting it right."

He brushed her lips again, then trailed ardent kisses along her jaw, across her cheeks.

She was lost. Her train of thought vanished as a will-o'-the-wisp. Alive with sensation, with her blood racing through her veins and her breathing hard to come by, she stepped even closer and shut her eyes when his mouth took hers in a searing kiss.

The stars outside dimmed in memory with the starburst that came. His lips were hot and compelling and she rose to the challenge, matching him kiss for kiss.

When his tongue skimmed over her lips, she opened them, shivering again at the delight that filled her. Pressing against his chest, she held on tightly, wishing the moment would go on forever.

He deepened the kiss and took her to the stars and beyond.

Sanity returned in short order.

"Don't pull away Arden," he muttered, kissing her eyes, her forehead, her cheeks again.

"We can't do this," she said breathlessly, resting her forehead against his chin, wishing she could let go of her inhibitions and let the moment take them where it would.

Releasing her hands, which had somehow become locked

behind his neck, she slowly drew them down and then pushed lightly against that rock-solid chest.

He released her instantly.

"Do you want me to apologize?" he asked.

She shook her head. "No. Never that."

Taking a deep breath, she moved to the counter, leaning against it gratefully. Her knees were too weak to hold her.

"Then?"

She wished the light was on so she could see him. But then he'd see her. Would he guess how his kisses had affected her? One look and she was sure the entire world would know.

"This can't go anywhere."

"It won't. It's just a few kisses." His tone was light.

"Then there's no point in tempting fate, is there?"

"And is it tempting?"

She shrugged, then realized he couldn't see her clearly.

"It could be," she said slowly. "I need to go to bed. I'm going to see my aunts again tomorrow."

"Running away?" he asked softly.

"Prudently stepping aside," she said.

Sidestepping to the opening to the family room, she turned and fled to her room as fast as she could.

She leaned against her closed door, reliving his kiss. Powerful and erotic, she still felt the tumbling sensations that made her feel like soft pudding inside.

Pushing away, she hurried to get to bed, determined to put

the last few minutes out of her mind and get to sleep.

She could hardly wait to see her aunts. Maybe discuss with them the problem she faced.

How could she be falling for a man who didn't want any involvement, and who if he ever married again, would want more children, especially sons?

But sleep didn't come quickly. Arden lay awake a long time, staring into the darkness, and trying to ignore the ache in her heart.

On Sunday, Arden spent the day with her aunts, but elected not to tell them about her feelings for Brendan. She already knew what they'd say. Hadn't she already planned for her future? Better to carry on with that than risk heartache by falling in love without being able to marry.

She stayed away until after she knew the girls would be asleep. Almost sneaking back into the house, she went directly to her room seeing no one. She heard Brendan moving around, but didn't call out. Thankfully, he wasn't in the family room.

Monday morning, she delayed going to the kitchen until she heard Hailey calling her. When she entered, the little girl was balanced on the counter, trying to pull down a box of cereal from one of the cupboards.

"What are you doing?" Arden asked, scooping her around the waist and swinging her to the floor.

"I was hungry, and you weren't here. Did you sleep in late?"

"A bit. Where's Avery?"

"She's watching Daddy get dressed. Can I eat now?"

Arden pulled down a bowl and went to the refrigerator for milk.

She wouldn't have minded watching their daddy dress. Or undress. What had he been wearing Saturday night?

She wished once again the lights had been on so she could have feasted her gaze on his physique. Her fingertips tingled in remembrance.

"He's leaving again on a trip," Hailey said, sitting at her place and watching as Arden prepared her bowl of cereal.

"I know. But just for a few days. You and Avery can paint on your mural and maybe have it finished by the time Daddy comes home."

Hailey nodded, engrossed in eating.

Brendan came into the kitchen carrying Avery just as the doorbell rang.

"That's probably my ride. I'm leaving the car here. Use it if you need it. The keys are o the table by the front door."

He deposited Avery in her chair and gave her a quick kiss. One for Hailey. Then he straightened and looked directly at Arden.

For a moment she saw the desire flare in his eyes. He wanted to kiss her goodbye as well.

She blinked and stepped back.

"I plan to be home on Wednesday."

With a curt nod, he left.

Arden stood transfixed. She heard him greet someone, and a couple of seconds later, the front door closed behind them. Silence, except for Hailey's spoon hitting the side of the bowl.

"Can I eat?" Avery asked, looking at Arden with puzzlement.

He couldn't have kissed her, not in front of the girls, she reasoned as she prepared Avery's breakfast.

But he'd wanted to. She knew it.

And she wouldn't have pushed him away this time.

By nine o'clock that night Arden knew Brendan wouldn't call. He hadn't said he would, but she remembered his nightly calls from Latin America. She had thought he might repeat the pattern from Washington.

Taking the baby monitor into her room, she sat down to study. Tomorrow was the first of her final examinations, and she was determined to do well. Of course, her project counted for a huge percentage of her grade in one course, but there would be a written test in all the courses.

Unfortunately, she couldn't concentrate.

She wondered what Brendan was doing. Had he taken his clients out to dinner? Wined and dined them as part of business?

Or did he just go with friends for fun and relaxation?

Was there a woman there he'd known for years, who might also have known Lannie? Someone he could talk to as an old friend?

Restlessly, she shifted on the bed, unable to focus on the words that danced in front of her. She wasn't paying attention.

Her phone rang.

She snatched it up.

"Hello?"

He'd called.

"Hi Brendan."

"Are the girls in bed?"

"Of course. It's after ten."

There was silence for a moment.

"Are you all right?" he asked.

She nodded, realizing he couldn't see her.

"Yes."

"Not your usual chatty self, however," he said with a trace of amusement.

"Which is probably a good thing. This way I don't talk your ear off."

"I wouldn't mind."

"Are things going all right there?" she asked.

"About as expected."

"I thought you might go out to dinner."

"I did. We finished a little while ago. That's why I'm late calling."

"I didn't know if you would call at all," she murmured.

"Didn't you want me to?"

She held her breath. Dare she admit it?

"Yes, I did," she said firmly.

He laughed softly at the other end.

"Why? After yesterday, I half expected you to let the call go to voice mail."

"Yesterday was my day off."

"So you needed to sneak back home last night?"

"I didn't sneak back," she protested.

"The only way I knew you were home was because I saw your car in the driveway."

Prudently, Arden remained silent. She had deliberately avoided him yesterday. Surely he knew why.

"Talk to me."

"About what?"

"Anything. Everything."

Gripping the receiver tightly, she asked the question that had plagued her since she arrived.

"Why are there no pictures of Lannie around for the girls?"

Chapter Twelve

S he heard his sharp intake of breath and wondered if she'd gone too far. But he'd said she could talk about anything.

"I put them all away after she died."

"She's been dead for three years. I think Hailey would like to see a picture of her mother. She asked when she saw the one I have of my mother on my dresser. She doesn't remember her, I think."

"That's not true. Of course she remembers her mom."

"Think about it. You don't talk about her. There aren't any pictures around. How could a little girl remember when there's nothing to jog her memory? Or keep her memories alive? And Avery had nothing to remember to begin with. I bet she'd love to see what her mother looked like."

He was silent.

Arden bit her lower lip, wondering if she'd gone too far. Had she made him angry? Sad?

"Brendan?"

"What?"

"Tell me something more about Lannie. What was she like? What was her favorite food, any movies she especially loved?"

"As you said, she's dead. What would be the point?"

"Maybe she's gone, but surely not forgotten. Not by you, nor should she be by her children. She was an important part of your life and of your children's lives. I want to know more about her."

"Why?"

To know what she was up against was her first thought. She brushed it aside.

"To help with the girls, of course. When something comes up, if I could say, you know your mother loved this, or hated this. Think how that could keep her memory alive for them."

"If you really want to know more about her, I'll tell you when I get home, but not tonight."

"Do you know when you'll be home?"

"Wednesday afternoon. I'll call you tomorrow."

She listened as he hung up and then tossed her phone beside her on the bed. Discussing Lannie was something she should have never brought up. She knew she'd heard the love in his voice when he spoke about her.

Would she ever hear such love when someone spoke about her?

Brendan hung up and rose from the hotel bed to walk to

the window. Washington sparkled in the night. The Capitol dome was illuminated for all the world to see. He leaned his forehead against the glass, the image before him fading as he tried to remember the very essence of Lannie.

It was harder and harder to do each day. He had to admit it had been ever since he interviewed a tall, leggy blonde.

Tuesday night, when her phone rang, Arden didn't answer it. She didn't want to talk to Brendan this evening.

Five minutes later, the house phone rang. After four rings, the answering machine picked up. The girls had already gone to bed, and she was finishing up cleaning the kitchen. She could easily hear the answering machine.

"Arden?" It was Brendan.

She listened, loved hearing his voice.

"Arden? It's Brendan. Pick up if you're there."

She clenched her hands into fists and refused to pick up the phone. It was necessary for her to maintain her distance. She'd thought about it long and hard. And tonight she'd start.

"Call me when you hear this."

A minute later, she pressed the play button on the machine to listen to him again. She loved his voice, the intonation, the deep, rich tones. Closing her eyes, she could see him as clearly as if he were standing in front of her.

She listened once more to the message, then switched off the kitchen light and went to check on the girls one last time before heading for her room.

The temptation to talk to Brendan was strong, but her resolve was stronger. She refused to be drawn in any deeper. She'd keep her distance and do her best to gain some perspective.

About an hour later, her phone rang again. Again, she ignored it.

She began the final study for another class, just skimming over her notes and the text. She'd done well during the semester, knew the material, and wasn't worried about how she'd do. But a last-minute brush-up couldn't hurt.

The house phone rang again. She held her breath, hearing the murmur of Brendan's voice on the machine in the kitchen.

Trying to concentrate, she did her best to ignore him. But the temptation to race to the phone was strong.

A few minutes later, the doorbell rang. Surprised, Arden glanced at the clock. It was after ten. Who came calling so late?

She went to the front door and peered through the glass panel on the side. A couple she recognized as living across the street stood on the porch.

She opened the door.

"Yes?"

"Are you Arden Glover?" the woman asked.

Arden nodded.

"Is everything all right here?" the man asked.

"Yes."

"Brendan Ferguson has been trying to reach you all night.

He's very concerned because no one is answering the phone. The girls are all right, aren't they?"

Arden felt horrible. She'd never thought about what Brendan might think when she didn't answer.

"We're all fine. The girls are in bed already."

The woman held out a scrap of paper.

"This is his cell phone number. He wants you to call him. He thought something might be wrong since he couldn't reach you."

Arden took the paper, guilt swamping her. Of course, Brendan would worry when she didn't answer. He knew she and the girls should be home. Not answering would definitely raise his concern. Why hadn't she thought about that? He must be frantic.

"I'll call him right away," she said.

"Better check the phone is working. We can wait. Must be something wrong if he can't get through," the man said. "You can come use our phone if you need to. Molly can stay with the girls."

"I'm sure it's fine. I'll come over if I can't reach him. You live in the yellow house, right?"

"That's right, Molly and Bill Dougans," Molly said brightly. "I've seen you here for several weeks but haven't had a chance to stop by. Welcome to the neighborhood. I understand you are watching the girls now that Ella has moved to California."

"That's right. Nice to meet you both. And thank you for coming over. I'll call Brendan now."

The couple left, and Arden closed the door.

What an idiot she was. Brendan was probably pacing his hotel room worried sick about his children and she'd deliberately not spoken to him when she should have.

Now what was she going to tell him?

She got her phone and quickly dialed him.

"Is everything all right there? I tried calling you several times. All I got was your voice mail or the answering machine."

"Everything's fine. I was, uh, studying. I have finals this week, you know. One tomorrow."

"You can't be too busy studying to pick up the phone and tell me you can't talk?"

She was silent. She should have done that.

"I didn't mean to have you worry. I'm sorry." There, she had to get that out.

"What's going on?"

She couldn't tell him. The last thing he'd want to hear was his children's nanny was falling for him. That she had to protect her heart the only way she knew. Yet what else would keep him from pressing her?

"Arden?"

"I really don't have time to talk, Brendan. I really need to study. Everyone is fine. The girls went to bed on time and we had a great day. The mural is almost finished. But I have to go now. Goodnight."

"Wait. Arden, what time is your final tomorrow?"

"Ten."

"Good, you'll be finished before three, right?"

"I'll be finished before noon. Why?"

"Can you pick me up at the airport? I'll be arriving at three o'clock on the flight in from Washington. Larry's staying on until Friday, so I need a ride home," he said, referring to the employee he'd made the trip with. He gave her the name of the airline he was flying.

"Okay, we'll be there. I have to go."

She hung up, her heart racing. He'd be home tomorrow. And then what? All efforts tonight to avoid hearing his voice were futile. What would she do when he was home again?

Arden and the girls arrived at the airport a few minutes past three. They stopped in front of the baggage claim area. She hoped she could stay until he came out. The airport police were strict on the no parking policy.

"Where's Daddy?" Hailey asked.

"He'll be coming out of one of these doors any minute now," she said. Arden had double checked the updated information for his flight and knew it was on time.

She felt anticipation rise as first one, then two and three people began walking out of the automatic doors.

Two businessmen hurried out, briefcases in hand.

A family.

Then Brendan.

He saw the car immediately and headed there.

"Hi, Daddy." Hailey called, waving.

"Daddy," Avery shrieked, laughing. "Did you come on an airplane? We saw airplanes flying!"

"I did. It landed a few minutes ago."

He put his carry-on bag in the trunk and opened the back door to lean over to kiss each daughter, giving them a hug.

He slid into the passenger side of the car and then, with a light in his eyes, he leaned over and kissed her firmly on the mouth.

Startled, she clung for a moment, savoring the contact, the racing of her heart, the feeling of being wild and romantic and on the edge of passion.

He released her and fastened his seat belt as if nothing monumental had happened.

Arden looked at him in confusion and sudden sadness.

She couldn't stay.

She couldn't be a part of his family, loving him the way she did.

She had to leave.

She started the car and focused on driving.

He'd be furious. She'd promised three years.

But if she told him why, he'd have to let her go.

In fact, if he had a clue she loved him, he'd probably fire her to save her the trouble of quitting.

"I missed you and the girls," he said.

She tried to smile, but felt the wobbly attempt wasn't very good.

"We missed you, too. Was it a successful meeting?"

She blinked her eyes, trying to clear the tears so she could see.

"Mostly. Larry's finalizing a few details, but the major points are taken care of."

She concentrated on her driving. She had to keep it together for a little longer.

For a moment Arden had felt as if they were a family, greeting the husband and father returning from a trip. Going to their home where they could shut out the world.

She wanted it so much that the longing was almost a physical pain.

It'd be so hard to leave. So hard to say goodbye.

"What have you three been up to? How did your exam go this morning?"

"I think I did well. I have the last exam on Friday morning."

"So you'll be carefree and ready to party Friday night," he said.

"Friday night?"

"The Andrews party. I asked you a while ago, remember? My plus one?"

She'd completely forgotten.

She couldn't go.

Could she?

It'd be one last night together, a memory to cherish down through the years.

"I remember. What time is it?"

"We'll leave around seven-thirty. Since you forgot, I expect you didn't get a babysitter?"

"No."

"Jamie Sue Morton used to watch the girls if both Ella and I needed to go out. She's in the address book in the drawer beneath the phone. I'll call her to see if she can watch them."

"It's short notice," Arden said. "If she can't, I could ask my aunts. They'd have to stay over. There's a curfew at their retirement home. They can't stay out to all hours and then show up. Stupid rules, if you ask me."

Brendan nodded, amusement glimmering in his eyes. "I think you mentioned those stupid rules before."

By the end of the week, Arden thought she'd imagined the kiss at the airport. Brendan had done nothing since he returned Wednesday afternoon to show he even remembered kissing her. He came home early Thursday and spent time with the girls before dinner. After they went to bed, he disappeared into his office.

Arden couldn't complain because it gave her time to study.

Not that she could concentrate. She spent most of the evening listening for him. If he came into the kitchen, she could go out for a glass of iced tea. If he watched television, she'd be able to see him through the opened door.

But he didn't come near her.

Friday, she finished her exams, picked the girls up at the university day care and headed for the mall at Military Circle. She had a dress to find for that night.

She wanted the perfect creation. One that would stay in Brendan's memory long after she'd gone.

She also wanted something that would give her the courage to tell him she was leaving. She'd go to the party, enjoy as much of it as she could, and then tell him when they returned home.

Of course, she wouldn't leave immediately. She'd give him time to find someone else. But the sooner he got started, the better.

And she had to look for another job, as well.

For a moment, doubt rose. Did she have to leave? Could she get over the feelings she had for Brendan without leaving?

She didn't think she'd ever get over falling in love. She'd never wanted a special man to share her life with. Knowing she could not have children, she'd resigned herself to a single life. Nothing had changed just because she'd fallen in love.

She'd tell him tonight.

"You look pretty, Arden," Hailey said, looking up at her

with a wide smile. Both girls had followed Arden to her room to watch her get dressed for the party.

"Are you a princess?" Avery asked.

"No, sweetie, same old Arden. And thank you, Haley, I'm glad you think so."

Arden looked into the mirror, turning from side to side to see as much as she could. She tried to quell the butterflies in her stomach. She did look nice. She hoped Brendan thought so.

The dress was perfect, a deep rose color, soft and feminine yet wildly sexy. It was short, showing off her long legs nicely displayed by the high heels.

Brendan was tall enough so she could wear the highest heels and still not be eye to eye with him.

She'd coaxed her hair into an elaborate style, piled on top of her head with wavy tendrils on either side of her face. It left her neck bare and showed off her dangling silver earrings perfectly.

"I'm pretty, too," Avery said, leaning close to the mirror, examining the makeup Arden had put on her.

Both girls had wanted to dress up. With loads of eye shadow and lipstick, they almost looked like clowns, but both thought they were perfect.

She wondered what Brendan would say. Maybe she should warn him to be complimentary.

"Ready?"

It was time. She'd heard Brendan arrive with the babysitter a few minutes ago.

They walked into the family room. Jamie Sue turned and greeted the girls. They ran over to her to show off their makeup. She was enthusiastic in complimenting each girl.

Brendan looked at Arden, his eyes darkening to deep silver as his gaze ran from her hair to her toes.

Arden flushed, feeling that fluttering inside again. She wished they were alone. Would he kiss her if they were?

Stop it, she admonished herself. She had to stop thinking about his kisses.

He introduced her to Jamie Sue, and then turned slightly to say softly,

"You look lovely."

Avery danced over to her father and smiled up at him.

"Aren't I pretty, Daddy?" She fluttered her eyelashes to make sure he could see the makeup.

Before Brendan could say a word, Arden reached out to touch his arm.

"Both girls decided to dress up like me. They're beautiful, aren't they?"

"Give me some credit," he murmured.

Stooping to Avery's level, he gravely studied her face, then smiled. "You are beautiful, honey. All dressed up. You look like a princess."

"Uh-huh. And me and Hailey are going to get dressed up

again. Next time, we'll have fancy dresses like Arden."

"I look forward to that."

"Can we go dancing?" Hailey asked, drawn to her sister's side.

"One day, when you're a little taller."

He stood up and looked at Jamie Sue. "Any questions? I left the usual information by the house phone, doctor's number, neighbor's number and, of course, my cell number."

"No, questions. We'll be fine. They're great kids. Have a nice time."

The Andrews party was at their stately old home in Ghent. Since parking in the area was difficult and they'd arranged valet service, so Brendan drove right to the front and gave the young man the keys.

The wide veranda that ran the width of the house was crowded with guests. Uniformed waiters circulated with beverages and hors d'oeuvres.

Brendan escorted Arden up the shallow steps and through the wide-open double doors. They greeted their hosts and then began to mingle with the other guests.

"Are you here for fun or business?" Arden asked when he appeared to be searching the crowd.

"Business. Large parties aren't my idea of fun."

"Oh, why not?"

He dropped his gaze to her.

"I prefer picnics in the backyard, or watching television

with my daughters."

"You'd have loved the beach last weekend."

"I already said I'll go next time."

For a moment Arden almost forgot there'd be no next time for her.

She smiled and looked away. She changed her mind. She wouldn't spoil tonight by announcing her departure. Time enough for that in the morning.

"Does your firm supply security for private homes or only offices and public buildings?" she asked.

"We do both. The Andrews have been clients for years. They were one of my first private homes. You'll like Cissy Andrews if you have time to visit with her. She'll talk your ear off, but she's funny and always kind. Ah, the very person I want to see."

He pressed his hand at the small of her back and guided her to a couple just arriving.

Before long, Arden was listening to Brendan and Lance Warwick discuss the ramifications of not using Brendan's company's services versus the expense. When the man's wife asked if Arden worked for Brendan, she explained the relationship.

Discovering Jenny Warwick had two young children, they were soon talking about summer activities appropriate for preschoolers.

Music drifted in from the back. Cissy Andrews joined

them, urging everyone to the backyard.

"We have an area for dancing. And the buffet tables are full, you'll get first pick."

She chatted briefly with Jenny and Arden, then moved on to another group.

The backyard was huge, with a canopy over the food tables to the left, a five-piece combo playing in the rear, complete with dance floor laid out near the band. Colorful Japanese lanterns illuminated every inch.

When Brendan asked her to dance, Arden felt excitement shimmer through her. It was a slow tune, and she moved into his arms without hesitation. She was here to make memories, and what better one than dancing with the man she loved?

Their steps meshed perfectly. She relaxed and enjoyed the movement, enjoyed the feeling of his arms around her, the feel of his muscular chest against hers, the scent of aftershave he'd splashed on.

"Are you enjoying yourself?" he asked, his voice soft in her ear.

Arden closed her eyes and imagined what it'd be like to be with him forever. To go to bed together and spend the night wrapped in each other's arms. To hear his voice in the darkness saying things only she would ever hear.

Nodding, she didn't want to break the spell. It was magic. Being with him, dancing, meeting his friends and acquaintances. Bittersweet memories, she thought with a pang, as she realized she wouldn't share this with him again.

"I've been thinking about what you said about Lannie and her pictures," he said after a moment.

Arden opened her eyes and pulled back enough to see his face. "What?"

"That Hailey and Avery need photos of their mother, so they'll know what she looked like to remember she was their mother."

She nodded. She cherished the photographs she had of her parents. It was so hard to remember them. If she didn't have the photographs, she knew she'd no longer be able to see their faces.

"Thursday night, I got the box down from the closet to choose a couple of photos. I'd packed them all away when she died. It was weird. I looked at them last night and it was easier than I thought it'd be," Brendan said.

Easier and yet difficult, he remembered. Lannie was young and pretty when she died. She'd been happy in their marriage, in the life they'd made together. At least he had that.

But Lannie was forever gone. It was time to move on.

He drew Arden closer, involuntarily comparing the two women.

Lannie had been much shorter. Arden was easier to dance with, their steps matching, her head resting against his cheek.

And the feelings he felt around Arden were different. She threw him more times than not with her outspoken views, her wild schemes and her zest for living. It shook him up.

And he needed that, he admitted. He'd kept a tight control on his emotions for three years. Almost depriving his children of their remaining parent.

Which brought up the thought of what if something happened to him? Who would love his daughters as he did? Who would take care of them and help them grow into womanhood?

He knew his parents would step in, or Ella. But maybe his children needed something different, something that Arden brought.

The song ended, and Arden stepped back, smiling up at him. Brendan had the strongest urge to kiss her. But not here, not during a party with a hundred guests or more.

When he kissed her, he wanted it to be in the privacy of their home.

He'd told her he didn't want an affair. But now he wondered if he'd known it was a lie. He wanted Arden Glover, and that surprised him to his core.

Chapter Thirteen

Arden awoke on Saturday morning in a wonderful mood. The party had been terrific. Dreamily, she remembered how she and Brendan had danced the night away. She'd met more people throughout the evening and found everyone friendly and easy to talk with. Brendan had seemed to enjoy himself as well.

The only awkward moment had been when he left to take home the babysitter. He'd asked her to wait up for him, but she'd fled to her room like a scared rabbit. She was in over her head and had to protect her heart the best way she knew how.

And a late-night tryst with Brendan Ferguson was not the way to do it.

Luxuriating in the free morning, she stretched and considered what she'd do today. School was over for the semester. For good or bad, she'd done her best on the exams. Now a lazy summer day beckoned. The entire weekend lay before her, but she had no plans, no burning desire to do anything.

She should tell Brendan about her decision to leave, but

the urgency she'd felt since that afternoon at the airport had eased. There was time enough to tell him on Monday. He couldn't do anything about locating a replacement over the weekend. Why worry him with the news before then?

Maybe she'd go to the library and check out some books and then head for the beach. Swimming, reading and maybe a nap sounded like the best way to spend a lazy day.

For a moment, the reality of leaving was almost overwhelming.

She'd grown to love Hailey and Avery. She'd miss them so much. Would another babysitter love them? Would someone else let them paint and encourage them to run and laugh? Or would they follow that strict regimen Ella had followed?

Pushing the disquieting thoughts away for the moment, she dressed in a sleeveless top and shorts. Sandals were all she needed. She'd kick them off when she reached the beach.

Heading for the kitchen a few minutes later, she noticed how late it was, after eleven. Of course, it had been late when they returned home, even so, the day was practically half gone.

She was amazed she hadn't heard the girls.

Where was everyone?

Glancing out the window, she saw Hailey and Avery playing in the sandbox, a pail of water beside them.

Hailey was fiercely concentrating on building a castle, using the water to soak the sand. Her tongue peeped from the corner of her mouth.

Avery haphazardly dug in the sand, piling up a mound, her attention to the task adorable.

They were chatting away, but Arden couldn't hear them. Were they remembering their day at the beach last weekend?

She dashed into her room and found her sketch pad. Grabbing a couple of charcoal pencils, she returned to the kitchen and began sketching the girls. Her book was almost full of sketches of the Ferguson family, from her fantasy drawings of Brendan as a Viking to different portraits of the girls. She knew it was the best work she'd ever done.

"Good morning." Brendan said behind her.

She spun around, startled at the sound of his voice. She hadn't heard him.

Brendan leaned against the doorjamb, watching her. His hands were in the pockets of his jeans, the pullover shirt he wore delineated the firm muscles of his shoulders and chest.

Arden could happily stare at him all day. Once again her fingers itched to sketch him. This time she'd draw him just as he stood, his confident male assurance contrasting with the casual pose.

Oh, how she was going to miss him.

"Hi."

"You slipped off to bed too early last night," he said.

Flustered, she tried not to show it.

"I was tired. I had a great time. Your friends are delightful."

"Did you eat any breakfast?"

She shook her head.

"It's so close to lunchtime, I'll just wait, then get something when I go out."

"Are you off to someplace now?"

"I'm going to the library."

She raised the sketch book and shrugged.

"Then I got sidetracked when I saw the girls in the yard. I wanted to capture the moment on paper."

"May I see?" he asked,

He pushed away from the wall and walked toward her. For a moment Arden almost forgot to breathe. Then she looked at the sketch. Would he like it?

Would he think she'd captured Hailey's serious concentration? That she'd contrasted the dainty daughters with their unique personalities?

"Sure." She held out the sketch pad.

For the first time, she questioned how she'd tell him about her decision to leave. He'd be disappointed she hadn't stayed the agreed-upon time.

The next time he needed to find someone who wouldn't make the mistake of falling in love with her boss.

"You're talented," he murmured as he studied the sketch and then gazed out in the yard at his daughters.

Flustered with the warm glow that spread with his praise, Arden stepped away. She was delighted he liked what she'd done, but standing too close wasn't wise. She longed to throw herself into his arms and demand he kiss her.

Wouldn't he be shocked if she did so?

"Want some coffee?" she asked, longing for something to do.

"Thanks, I'd like that."

She turned to fill the coffeemaker but hearing the rustle of paper, she spun around. Too late. He was already looking at her other sketches.

"No, don't."

She almost ran across the room, but Brendan ignored her, studying the drawing of the mighty Viking warrior with his body and face.

He flipped over to another page and found the one she'd dreamed about for several nights. Brendan in bed, a bunched up sheet cutting across the lower part of his body, his muscular chest and arms revealed as he gazed at an unseen lover. In her mind, she'd been the woman he looked at so hungrily.

Arden froze, wishing the floor would open up and swallow her whole.

She reached out to snatch the pad from Brendan, but he swiveled around, putting his body between her and the pad. He flipped to another page and another.

Suddenly, he lowered the tablet and looked at her. His eyes were hot and watchful.

Arden didn't know what to do, but she couldn't look away from the heat in his gaze. She licked her lips nervously and his gaze honed on the movement like a hawk.

"These are interesting," he said slowly. "Once you said you were good at art but not super. I think you're too critical. I'd call these drawings excellent."

"Assignments for school," she offered lamely, relishing his compliment.

Slowly, Brendan shook his head.

"I don't think so."

Unerringly, he flipped to the Viking warrior pose and held it out to her. "This one?"

She swallowed, her eyes staring at the imaginative rendition. It was one of her best drawings.

He flipped to the one showing the resting warrior with the two small girls in a garden, the one she'd wanted to do in oils.

The silence stretched out. What could she say?

"Arden, there's something I wanted to discuss with you last night, but you disappeared before I came back from taking Jamie Sue home. Now I think it was meant that we waited"

"Oh?"

She cleared her throat nervously. She couldn't think when they were so close. Turning, she looked out the window. The girls were still industriously playing in the sandbox, but Arden didn't see them. Her heart pounded, and she knew embarrassed color stained her cheeks.

Clearing her throat, she asked, "What did you want to talk about?"

He ran the fingers of one hand through his hair. Tossing the sketchpad on the counter, he crossed his arms over his chest.

"I'm not sure how to begin."

She blinked in surprise. She never thought she'd hear Brendan sounding the least bit unsure.

Oh dear, was he going to fire her? Had he recognized the pictures for what they were, the fantasy of a woman in love?

She almost laughed. Here she planned to resign on Monday and he was about to fire her today. She should have stuck to her original schedule.

She met his gaze, wishing she'd spoken first.

"You seem to like the girls," he began.

She nodded. "I love them. They're adorable. You've done a great job raising them. I suspect you'll continue to do so."

"As long as I'm around."

"What do you mean?"

A touch of panic unexpectedly hit her.

"You aren't sick, are you? You don't have some life-threatening disease?"

"No. But life's uncertain. They've already lost one parent. I worry about what would happen to them if something happens to me."

"Well, I'm sure nothing will. And in the unlikely event

something did, your parents are a phone call away. And Ella would step in."

He shook his head.

"My parents are too old to take on two rambunctious little girls. I wouldn't want Hailey and Avery to have to live with older parents."

"Ella," she said, wondering why he was bringing this up.

He shrugged.

"Actually, I thought that it'd be best if something happened to me for the girls to stay in the house, in familiar surroundings. Kept their same routines."

Arden nodded, wondering where this was leading.

"I want you to be their guardian if anything happens to me. Give them the continuity and love they'll need."

She stared, dumbfounded.

"You want me to be the girls' guardian if something happens to you?" she repeated.

"Money wouldn't be an issue. I'd see to that. They adore you. You bring a fresh outlook to their lives. One I can see has made a very positive difference. They are happy and enthusiastic about every new experience you bring them."

"Brendan, you're probably going to live to be a hundred. You don't need me to be a guardian."

This conversation wasn't going at all like she expected.

It was time to tell him she was leaving.

"But in case I don't make it to one hundred, would you

think about it, Arden? About becoming part of this family and being there for them?"

"I guess I could think about it," she floundered.

He paused for a heartbeat, then said, "It'd simplify things if we got married."

"Married?"

A spurt of joy hit before reality reasserted itself. The absolutely last thing to do that would simplify things.

Blood rushed through her, the pounding of her heartbeat sounding inordinately loud in her ears. She couldn't think, could feel nothing beyond a stunned numbness.

Brendan Ferguson was suggesting they get married.

In that second, she figured out he wasn't planning to fire her.

"I was going to quit," she said, bewildered.

"Quit? What are you talking about?"

"I, uh, nothing. My mind is blank. I can't marry you."

He studied her, his eyes narrowed.

"I mean, you can't want to marry me," she said sadly.

"I wouldn't have brought it up if I didn't," he said evenly. "And after seeing the drawings, I suspect you don't feel totally indifferent to me."

She broke eye contact, and looked around the kitchen wildly, as if searching for something that would guide her, give her the proper words to respond.

Marry him.

As in live with him forever?

She loved him. How could she not wish to spend the rest of her life with him?

But he didn't love her. The sketches she'd done showed only *her* feelings.

He hadn't even hinted at any emotional attachment on his part. Would she be just a substitute wife, someone to take care of his children?

She shook her head. He obviously didn't know one important fact that would have him rescinding that crazy proposal in a heartbeat.

"I can't have children," she blurted out.

He looked taken aback.

"I didn't know that. Do you want children? More, I mean, than Avery and Hailey?"

"Of course not. They are wonderful. But men want sons."

"You say that as if it's a law or something."

"I know men want sons. I've heard it all my life. Sons to do things with, to relate to man to man. You said so yourself. You said you'd relate better to boys. And you need a son to carry on the family name."

He stepped right up to her, crowding her back against the counter. He rested a hand on either side of her hips, effectively capturing her within his arms, yet not quite touching.

Arden felt as if the air whooshed from the room. She gazed up at him helplessly. It was too much to hope for, but she couldn't extinguish the small flickering flame deep inside.

"I already have two wonderful children. Lannie and I didn't plan to have any more. I don't see that as a problem."

"But a son. You don't have a son."

"What's wrong with girls?"

"*Nothing.* But all my life, I've heard how sad it was my folks didn't have a son, that my dad didn't have a boy to follow in his footsteps, to carry on the family name. My aunts still talk about it to this day."

Brendan stared into her eyes for a moment, then said, softly, "So maybe your folks wanted a boy. But I bet they loved their little girl. They didn't want a boy instead of you, just in addition, right?"

Arden thought back. He was right. She'd heard them say another baby would be wonderful. But she'd never heard anyone express the wish that she'd been a boy.

Even her aunts had said there should have been more children. More, not instead of.

"I guess. But,"

"Is that the reason you said you'd never marry? Because you couldn't have kids?"

She nodded, her throat closing up, her heart beat raggedly. Could he possibly still want to talk about marriage? Despite her inability to have children, was he still interested?

"That's not an issue with us. We'll have the girls. And I have two brothers who can carry on the family name. That was never my goal in life."

Hope blossomed. There was still so much to overcome. Could she do it? Could she marry a man she loved, knowing he loved a dead woman?

"So you want us to marry so Hailey and Avery would have a new mother," she clarified.

Brendan hesitated, his eyes staring deeply into hers. Was that desire she saw? Or only a projection of her own feelings?

"Not exactly."

"What then, *exactly?*" she demanded.

She felt sheltered standing in his arms. She wished he'd kiss her. She didn't have to think when he kissed her, only feel.

What was she going to do? Follow her heart? Or her head? Today's decision would impact the rest of her life.

How could she say no?

Yet, could she say yes?

"I want a wife. I want *you* for my wife, Arden."

Tears filled her eyes. If only he meant that.

"Don't cry. I didn't mean to make you cry," he said softly. "If the thought of being my wife is so repugnant, we'll come up with an alternate plan."

She smiled through her tears. "That sounds so business-like, an alternate plan."

"You can still get your degree, find a great job wherever you like. We'll work it out. Arden don't cry. It tears me up inside. I'll do whatever you want."

"Could you love me?" she said forlornly.

Oh, no. Had she said the words aloud?

Brendan froze, his eyes blazing down at her. "What did you say?"

"Nothing, I said nothing."

She wished the floor would open up and swallow her whole. Could she duck under his arm and run for her life and never look back?

"One thing I thought I'd have to do was give enough time, so maybe you'd come to care for me as much as you care for my daughters," Brendan said slowly. He dropped his arms to draw her into a warm embrace.

"But seeing these sexy pictures you drew, I knew I didn't need to wait. I'm not sure how it happened, but the woman who drew those pictures isn't indifferent."

She shook her head. Was she dreaming? Would she waken in a little while and find herself alone in her bedroom?

"I love you, Arden Glover. I want you for my wife. I want you in all the ways a man wants a woman."

"But you love Lannie," she protested.

"Yes, I loved her a lot. I'll always have a sweet spot in my heart for her. But she's gone. And you're here. Beautiful, talented, warm and loving. And so outrageous sometimes I'm constantly amazed and enthralled. Your kisses drive me wild. Your sunny disposition brings light to a routine existence. Your enchantment with life warms my heart. Everything about you entices me. There's so much I want to explore with you. Like see this pretty hair spread out on a pillow or feel the silky strands flow over my fingers. Like hearing your laughter each day. It makes my heart catch when I hear it. I want you to look at me with the love that shines in your eyes when you look at my daughters. I want to see you in the morning and at night and in between. And to grow old together. I want it all, Arden. And I want it with you."

"You said you didn't want to remarry."

She couldn't think. But hadn't he said that? Why was she bringing it up? He'd just said he loved her. She should latch on to that.

"I felt that way when Lannie died. I will never take you for granted. There'll always be a fear in me that something terrible will happen to you. But I need to take that chance. Otherwise, I know you'll leave, eventually. And that's what I can't bear. I want you in my life from now on forever."

"Forever?"

She leaned against him, hugging him tightly, the tears spilling down her cheeks.

"Oh, Brendan, I love you so much. I was going to quit and leave because I couldn't stand falling more and more in love and thinking I had no chance at a happy ending."

"So does that mean your answer is yes?" he demanded, his arms hugging her close.

"Yes. Yes!"

She laughed with joy.

"I can't believe this. Ten minutes ago, I was planning how to tell you I was leaving. Now I'm staying and getting married. Getting a family I never thought I'd have. Oh, Brendan, one day I'll even get grandchildren. You really love me? I'm not second best?"

"Oh, darling, never. I adore you, everything about you. I fought it. My intention was to keep my distance, keeping you segregated as an employee. But I couldn't."

"You aren't really worried anything will happen to you, are you?" she asked suspiciously.

He smiled slowly, shaking his head. "That was the only excuse I could come up with. I thought if you and I got married, eventually things would work out. I was counting on kisses and lovemaking to win you over."

"No need. You won me over with that first phone call from Latin America. It just took me a few days to realize it. Then I worked hard to make sure you never suspected."

"You could have given me a hint," he said with a smile.

"Ever since I had that infection as a teenager that prevents me from ever having children, I'd put marriage out of my plans for the future. I was going to be a dedicated career woman."

"If you want to work, go for it. If you want to paint for sheer pleasure, do that. Just love me and my girls, that's all I ask."

"Then you ask little, Brendan. Nothing you don't already have. I love you with all my heart and soul. I'll make you the best wife in the world."

"Just be yourself, sweetheart. That will make you the best in the world."

"Best wife," she corrected.

"No, the best, period."

She would have said more, but his kiss cut off the words. Her heart swelled with love as her arms tightened around his neck.

There were a million details to work out. Would the girls accept her? Would his family? What would the aunts say?

But Arden knew everything would work out. She knew she was where she belonged in Brendan Ferguson's arms. Forever, he'd said.

It just might be long enough.

Did you enjoy this story?
If so, you may enjoy MARRIAGE MASQUERADE,
Book Three in the Making a Family Series.

For a complete list of Barbara's books, visit her website at:
www.barbaramcmahon.com/books.

If you liked TEXAS TEMPTATION book,
please consider leaving a review.

www.ingramcontent.com/pod-product-compliance
Lightning Source LLC
Chambersburg PA
CBHW070019260626
47159CB00005B/1869